FOOL'S MATE

FOOL'S MATE
RITCHIE PERRY

PANTHEON BOOKS, NEW YORK

LIBRARY OF CONGRESS CATALOGING IN PUBLICATION DATA

Perry, Ritchie, 1942-
Fool's mate.

I. Title.
PR6066.E72F6   1981   823'.914   81-47210
ISBN 0-394-51916-7   AACR2

Manufactured in the United States of America
First American Edition

FOOL'S MATE

NAKASERO HILL, UGANDA, APRIL 1979

Although most of the cells were empty when the soldiers arrived, they had clearly been in use until the last possible moment. Pools of blood, some of it no more than twenty-four hours old, had coagulated on the floors. Human excrement was everywhere. In one of the cells bloody hand-prints on the wall marked a prisoner's painful struggle to pull himself upright. Further along the same corridor another prisoner had scrawled a final, defiant message, leaving it to be found by the Tanzanian and Ugandan National Liberation Front soldiers. 'GOD BLESS OUR CHILDREN AND BROTHERS WHO ARE STILL ALIVE' was what he had written, a message Kironde found particularly apt.

For the time being it was impossible to make any kind of accurate body count but it was already apparent that the victims numbered several hundred. Most of the bodies which remained had been discovered in one of the main chambers of the L-shaped State Research Bureau building. Scores of corpses lay there, as carelessly discarded as the pornographic magazines and electronic toys which littered the presidential mansion above. Amin's men hadn't intended to leave anybody alive who might be able to testify against them in the courts of the new regime.

The final executions had necessarily been hurried but they had been none the less methodical for this. The SRB butchers had had seven long years to perfect their techniques and they had kept to established routines. Each batch of victims had been forced to lie in the wide gutter which ran along the centre of the room. This was so that their blood could drain away without staining the bare concrete floor when they were hacked to death. The next

batch had then piled their predecessors' corpses against
the wall before taking their own turn in the drainage gutter. Sometimes this barbaric death hadn't been considered sufficient punishment. Many of the bodies bore
the unmistakable scars of torture. Others had been
savagely mutilated after they were dead.

At the far end of this room was a massive, locked door,
barring access to a second, larger chamber which extended beneath the presidential mansion. According to
reliable reports, several hundred more corpses lay inside.
So far, however, there had been no serious attempt to
blast the door open. Explosives and ammunition might be
stored there as well and the officers in charge didn't want
to risk destroying the building. If Kironde and his friends
had any say in the matter, the complex had to be pre-
served for posterity. It would be Uganda's Dachau, a permanent reminder of what life had been like under the
rule of President for Life Idi Amin.

Despite his hatred for the deposed dictator, Kironde
had been less affected by the nightmarish contents of the
SRB headquarters than most of the others who had arrived with him. He certainly hadn't been one of those who
had rushed outside to be sick. Kironde had witnessed the
evidence of too many other atrocities on the long march
from the Tanzanian border to be particularly surprised
by the discovery. In any case, he had never been one of
those Ugandans who had blinded themselves to what had
been happening for the past seven years. He had known
of the thousands of unnamed corpses which had been
thrown into the Nile to feed the crocodiles. He had heard
of the hundreds of unmarked mass graves which dotted
the entire country. He had always recognized Amin for
the monster he was.

What he could see there in the SRB headquarters was
merely the tip of the iceberg. Three hundred thousand
dead was one of the more conservative estimates. Three

hundred thousand of his countrymen wantonly slaughtered to satisfy the bloodlust of a semi-literate madman. Among them had been Kironde's father, mother, wife and sisters. As he stood there in the doorway, smoking a cigarette in a vain attempt to mask the smell of death, Kironde was adding more fuel to the hatred which had sustained him for the past five years. He didn't even turn his head when he heard footsteps approaching behind him.

'Well?' he said curtly.

'We've found half a dozen prisoners who are still alive,' Kibunka reported. 'They were in one of the last cells we forced open.'

'What condition are they in?'

Kironde had turned and he could see the tears glistening in his friend's eyes.

'Bad.' By now the tears were running free and unchecked down Kibunka's cheeks. 'They hadn't been fed at all for the last two weeks. None of them was making a great deal of sense but it seems they kept alive on the flesh of cellmates who died.'

Kironde nodded, his face totally impassive. He had forgotten how to cry a long time before.

'The tide has turned now,' he said, aware that he was talking in platitudes. 'They'll be hunted down, Amin, Astles, every last one of them. None of them will be allowed to escape.'

The words might be trite but the emotions behind them were frighteningly real. This mission was all that Kironde had left in life. It had been ever since one dreadful night five years before when he'd had to watch helplessly while Amin's thugs had butchered his family in front of his eyes.

Kironde's family had died because his father had believed what he had heard on Radio Uganda. His own intel-

ligence reports, or the very lack of them, should have
warned him that the coup had failed, that it was time for
him to cross the lake into Kenya. Instead he had listened
to Tennessee Ernie Ford and he had remained. The
broadcast of Onward Christian Soldiers was supposed to
have been the signal that Amin had been overthrown. In
fact it was simply the last in an apparently endless succes-
sion of mistakes. Amin had had no need for the immor-
tality he sometimes claimed when the plots against him
were so inept.

The abortive coup had been sparked by the discovery
of Lieutenant Colonel Michael Ondonga's bullet-riddled
corpse in the Nile. As Foreign Minister he had been the
highest ranking Lugbara in the Ugandan government
and his murder had been a message his fellow tribesmen
had been unable to ignore. The honeymoon with Amin
was over and their turn had come. Until Ondonga's death
the Lugbaras had desperately tried to blind themselves to
reality. They had refused to acknowledge the true signifi-
cance of key Lugbara officers disappearing without a
trace and of the dozens of others locked in Makindye
prison, charged with conspiracy. Now facts had to be
faced. Amin and the Muslim Kakwas had no more love
for the Lugbaras than they had for the Acholi or Langi.

Although Kironde and his father were Kakwas themselves, neither of them had had any hesitation in accept-
ing the conspirators' invitation to join the coup. Even
then, in March 1974, there had been too many bloody
purges for them to have had any illusions about the
monster who ruled their country. The sooner Amin was
gone, the sooner sanity would return to Uganda. Kironde
Senior, a Colonel in the army, had restricted himself to a
passive role, as he still considered himself bound by the
oath of loyalty he had sworn to the President. He had
promised the conspirators he wouldn't use the troops
under his command to defend the regime but he had

refused to play any active part in the insurrection.

The younger Kironde had had no such reservations. He had volunteered to be a member of the assassination squad which should have ambushed the President at his house on Kampala's Kokolo Hill, and no blame for the subsequent fiasco could be attached to him. His unit had reached the house at the designated time. His men had dealt with the guards who had been assigned to them as targets. It was no fault of Kironde's that the man they were looking for hadn't been at home. Perhaps Amin had been out searching for a new wife or two, replacements for the three he had divorced only the previous day.

Even with Amin alive, the coup could still have been successful, but the main Lugbara force had virtually guaranteed its failure. To begin with, everything had gone like clockwork. They had used their commandeered tank to blast down the main doors of the Malire mechanized battalion in Kampala. Inside, in the armoury, they had found all the weapons they needed. If they had then proceeded as planned and occupied other strong points in the capital, the coup might have maintained its momentum. Unfortunately the Lugbara leaders had allowed their hearts to overrule their brains. They had elected to head directly for the Makindye prison where they had released those of their colleagues who had been imprisoned there. This had given Amin all the time he had needed to gather a force of loyal troops around him and launch a decisive counterattack.

Young Kironde had continued fighting until he heard that Brigadier General Arube, the former chief of staff and the most influential member of the conspirators, had been killed. Then he had known it was time to throw away his weapons and concentrate on escape. He had intended to live to fight another day. It was only on the perilous journey back to his parents' home that he had begun to suspect the truth, that he and his fellow conspirators might have fallen into a trap which Amin had set for them. Only then did he consider the possibility that Ondonga's murder might have been a deliberate attempt to provoke the Lugbaras into insurrection.

However, this was a train of thought which Kironde had been unable to complete until much later. The three jeeps of the Public Safety Unit had passed him while he was still half a mile from his house and he had started to run, hoping against hope that his family had already fled to the border. The hours which had followed, after Kironde had discovered that his prayers hadn't been answered, had determined the whole future course of his life. What Kironde had witnessed, looking down from the flat roof of the outhouse into the main room of his parents' bungalow, had left no room in him for any emotion apart from an almost pathological hatred. Despite his horror and revulsion, Kironde had carefully filed away every last grisly detail. They were to be his justification for what he intended to do once he returned to his homeland as a free man.

CHAPTER 1

At four o'clock in the morning my biorhythms were way down, foundering at the bottom of a deep trough. Besides, I'd no way of knowing how many might be waiting for me inside my flat, any more than I knew what they wanted. There had been a time when I'd have sailed in regardless, driven on by the spirit of adventure, but this was one of the follies of youth I'd cured myself of during adolescence. As soon as I saw the curtains of the flat had been drawn, I changed my mind about parking outside and drove another couple of hundred yards around the corner before I stopped. Fortunately nobody had told the local vandals that the GPO had repaired the phone box for the third time that week. Either that or they were too busy mugging old-age-pensioners and immigrants to be bothered.

'It's Philis,' I announced once I was through to the duty officer. 'Somebody has broken into my flat.'

'Relax,' Randall told me. 'It isn't your night to be stomped by cuckolded husbands. When we couldn't reach you, we sent Gregson round.'

I found him snoring on the sofa, a glass and the remains of my bottle of Grant's handily placed on the table beside him. Most of the ice in the bucket had already melted but I managed to find a couple of lumps of ice which fitted quite nicely into his open mouth.

'You bastard, Philis,' he spluttered appreciatively when he'd finished choking. 'That wasn't funny.'

'It was from where I'm standing,' I told him. 'Anyway, we're wasting time. Tell me why you're here, then I can catch up on some beauty sleep.'

It only took Gregson ten minutes to pass on what little he knew and I spent another quarter of an hour going through the documents he'd brought with him. In the morning I'd have to go through them again and commit them to memory. By eleven o'clock I'd not only have to pretend to be somebody I wasn't, I'd be expected to know all the background appropriate to my new status in life.

'Exactly how solid is this cover?' I asked.

The face Gregson pulled was all the answer I needed. It was a rush job and with rush jobs there never was time for adequate preparation.

'Let's just say you'll be vouched for, Philis. If anybody bothers to do any real digging, you'll be up there without a paddle. You know how it is.'

I did, all too well. I'd have to be very careful not to raise any doubts.

'This Thackeray character,' I said. 'What do you know about him?'

Gregson shrugged.

'Not much more than I've already told you. He figures as vice-president in a couple of Sir Keith's companies but there's a lot more to him than that. He's Sir Keith's troubleshooter. You can make your own interpretation of what that means.

There was no need to ask about Sir Keith Tenby himself. I could read about him in the financial pages almost any morning. However, this did nothing to explain why Pawson was so eager to volunteer my services.

'You say you have no idea what the job involves?'

'I don't think Pawson has himself, although he could probably make an educated guess. All I'm supposed to tell you is that Thackeray has been making noises in rather strange areas and you fit the bill of what he's apparently looking for. It's down to you to take it from there.'

There was no point in questioning Gregson further. He didn't have any answers and Pawson, the man who did, evidently considered I had everything I needed. I wasn't sure I agreed with him but I'd discover which of us was right later in the morning. All I could do for now was grab as much sleep as possible before I crossed my fingers and jumped in at the deep end.

Even when the needle flickered above the hundred mark, Thackeray handled the Porsche with almost contemptuous ease. I suspected that this was how he did most things in life. Although he'd spoken no more than a dozen words since he'd picked me up, I'd already classified him as somebody to be reckoned with. It was no coincidence that so many products of the public school system had found their way into the various security units and, despite what a lot of people seemed to think, this had little to do with the old school tie. Public schools seemed to develop a confidence and self-reliance which couldn't be matched by the State schools and Thackeray struck me as a perfect example of this. He might have opted for private enterprise but he had several of the hallmarks of a top professional. I guessed that Sir Keith Tenby had chosen wisely and well.

The country club was a few miles outside Guildford, with a high brick wall which was admirably designed to show how exclusive it was. In Thackeray's company, however, I had no problems about admission. He merely had to toot his horn and one of the club's lackeys was scrambling to open the impressive wrought-iron gates. Thackeray even merited a salute which he acknowledged casually before he started down the drive. The club buildings formed quite an impressive complex beside the golf course and we obviously had the place to ourselves. I could detect no signs of activity inside the clubhouse, the golf course was having a rest day and the Porsche was the only vehicle in the car park apart from a solitary Rolls. I couldn't believe this was normal for a summer Sunday.

'Business doesn't look too good,' I commented as I opened the door.

'It doesn't, does it?' Thackeray agreed.

Once we were out of the car I could appreciate just how big Thackeray was, although this wasn't what impressed me most. He might be at least six feet four, with the kind of muscular development I normally associated with body-building ads, but there was nothing muscle-bound about the way he moved. He didn't go very far, only to the boot of the Porsche, but this was plenty far enough for him to reinforce the impression of total coordination he'd given while he was driving. Beyond any shadow of a doubt, Thackeray had been designed as one of nature's predators, and female prey was never going to be hard for him to come by. Facially, he resembled a young Paul

Newman, with eyes so blue they were almost opaque in the bright sunlight.

The weapons were in a special compartment which had been built into the boot of the Porsche and there were three of them. The Uzi he tossed casually across to me. The Smith and Wesson .38 and the FN light automatic rifle Thackeray kept for himself, together with a string bag containing the ammunition.

'What are we going to do?' I asked. 'Declare war?'

'Not quite.' Thackeray had a good smile, backed up by the kind of white, even teeth I'd have thought were capped if they'd been in anybody else's mouth. 'I learned a long time ago never to take anything on trust.'

I grunted and followed Thackeray across to a long, low building which stood slightly apart from the main clubhouse. It came as no great surprise to discover it housed a range. Acting on Thackeray's instructions, I fired off a couple of magazines from the Uzi and about two dozen rounds from the revolver, making pretty patterns in the man-sized targets somebody had thoughtfully provided. Although I shot well, I took care not to shoot as well as I could. Any real marksmanship and Thackeray might have started wondering exactly who it was he was hiring.

'What about the rifle?' I enquired.

'You can use that outside,' Thackeray told me. 'It will give me a better idea of what you can do.'

Another target had been set up in one of the deeper bunkers on the golf course and it was far enough away for me to settle into the Bisley-approved firing position. I loosed off one clip at single-shot and another on automatic while Thackeray watched how I was doing through the range telescope he'd brought with him.

'OK?' I asked. 'Or do you have any other little games to keep us amused?'

I wasn't making any secret of the fact that I hadn't entered into the true spirit of things.

'We're just about finished now,' Thackeray answered easily, electing to overlook my resentment. 'At least we've established that you can shoot.'

'Like hell you have,' I retorted. 'Making holes in pieces of cardboard isn't shooting. It only counts when the target is shooting back.'

Although he didn't answer, Thackeray looked as though he agreed with me. It wouldn't have surprised me one little bit to discover he knew all about using a gun on a human target.

Once the weapons had been returned to the boot of the car, Thackeray indicated that we should head for the clubhouse. I received my first warning when I caught a brief flash of movement behind the windows of the bar. Confirmation came a second or two later when Thackeray allowed me to move slightly ahead of him. I thought I knew what was about to happen but there didn't seem to be any alternative to playing the sucker. The most I could do was ensure I didn't bruise myself on the tarmac after Thackeray had kicked my feet from under me.

'What the hell?' I began indignantly, pushing myself up off the ground.

I never finished what I had to say because Thackeray kicked me in the stomach while I was halfway up. He didn't put his full weight behind his foot, thank God, but it connected hard enough to knock me down and he kicked me again before I could roll clear. By the time I was on my feet, Thackeray was crowding me, delivering a flurry of punches and chops which kept me fully occupied, with the occasional kick thrown in for good measure. Although he was mixing his attack quite nicely, showing he was even faster on his feet than I'd expected him to be, I wasn't in one of my more appreciative moods. While none of his blows was intended to really damage me, they weren't designed to do me a great deal of good either. It was only a few seconds before my forearms and biceps were becoming bruised from the punches I'd blocked.

It was the bloody arrogance of the man which really got up my nose. Thackeray was so sure of himself. He thought he was good enough to play his little game with me without any risk to himself, and this was what decided me that he was due for a lesson. Although I couldn't blow my cover by going into one of the routines I'd been taught at the SR(2) training school, there was no harm in Thackeray learning how sneaky I was. This involved a bit more pain when I deliberately allowed one of his punches to catch me in the stomach, and once I was down, I stayed down. I didn't even take evasive action when Thackeray kicked me. I simply remained in my foetal position and practised a moan.

'Come on, Philis,' Thackeray sneered. 'Surely you can do better than that.'

He wasn't even out of breath.

'For Christ's sake, you crazy bastard,' I moaned, still clutching myself. 'You've busted something inside.'

'Don't be stupid.' To emphasize his point Thackeray kicked me yet again. 'I've hardly touched you.'

I tried a few more groans to prove I didn't believe him and I could sense Thackeray's contempt growing as he stood above me. His test had turned sour and he abruptly lost patience with me.

'Come on,' he said, bending down to grab hold of me. 'You can't lie there all day.'

This was what I'd been waiting for and I came on, far faster than Thackeray had anticipated. He was only just beginning to realize his mistake in offering to help me up when my knee caught him between the legs and he had a bit more to think about a fraction of a second later after my head had connected with the bridge of his nose. Suddenly Thackeray discovered he was the one down on the tarmac and I didn't allow him an opportunity to recover. With the sole of my right shoe resting none too lightly on his larynx, I was firmly in control.

'Bat an eyelid and you'll be talking with a croak for the rest of your life,' I told him.

Although Thackeray did start to say something, he changed his mind when I put a bit more pressure on his throat. There were several ways he could move my foot but he had the sense not to want to try any of them. He hadn't been looking for a serious contest when he'd first tripped me and he certainly didn't intend to risk any permanent damage simply to prove a point. This would have been rather stupid when he had somebody standing by to bail him out.

'That will be enough, Philis,' Sir Keith Tenby said from behind me, standing in the clubhouse door. 'There's no need for anybody to be hurt.'

I went through all the motions of being surprised by his intervention but I was relieved that Sir Keith had decided to show his hand. If he hadn't, I wasn't quite sure what I'd have done with Thackeray. It said in all the best fairy stories that you weren't supposed to kill the goose who laid the golden eggs.

Thackeray showed another side to himself once I'd allowed him up from the ground. There was a fair quantity of blood coming from his nose, and my knee hadn't done him any good either, but he didn't appear to be particularly resentful. On the contrary, he seemed to be pleased with the way I'd handled myself, and Sir Keith was almost painfully eager to pour oil on any troubled waters. I maintained my own mock anger long enough to be ushered inside the clubhouse and fed a large whisky. Then I gradually began to simmer down.

'It was necessary to see precisely what you could do,' Thackeray explained. 'It could be very important.'

'And you shouldn't blame Tom for what happened, either,' Sir Keith added. 'It was all my fault. He was acting under my specific instructions.'

'That's all very well,' I pointed out, 'but I came here looking for a job. I was under the impression that I was already vouched for.'

'You were, Mr Philis, you were.' Sir Keith's manner suggested he was well accustomed to soothing disgruntled stockholders. 'Your references were excellent. Unfortunately, what we have in mind is far too delicate for anything to be left to chance.'

'The word mercenary can cover a multitude of sins,' Thackeray chipped in, taking time off from dabbing at his nose, and managing a not unfriendly smile. 'We have to be absolutely certain we have the right man.'

'It's not all one-sided,' I pointed out. 'I don't know yet that I'll be interested in what you have to offer. So far you haven't given me any idea of what I might be expected to do.'

Thackeray and Sir Keith exchanged quick glances. I wasn't pushing hard but I was definitely pushing and this was something they didn't want.

'That comes later,' Sir Keith said. 'First of all there are one or two questions we want to ask you.'

'You'll understand why soon enough,' Thackeray contributed, quick to forestall any possible objections on my part. 'The fewer details you know at the moment, the easier it will be for either party to back off in the event we can't agree.'

I'd learned all about the need to know theory from Pawson and I hadn't missed the faint threat implicit in what Thackeray had just said. This seemed as good a reason as any for being cooperative and not doing any more pushing for the moment. To begin with the questions were routine, concentrating on the career of my assumed persona, and I didn't have any problems in coming up with satisfactory answers. It was left to Thackeray to probe a little deeper.

'There are several quite lengthy gaps in your employment record,' he said. 'I see one of them lasted for over a year. How do you account for that?'

'Us mercenaries are like actors,' I explained. 'We often spend a lot of time in between jobs.'

'And that's all there is to it?'

My answer obviously hadn't completely satisfied Thackeray.

'Not quite.' I hoped neither of them had read any books by John D. MacDonald. 'It's always seemed stupid to me to wait until you're old and past it before you pack up work. I try to take my retirement in stages as I go along. I'm paid well while I'm working. Then I live off the proceeds until the coffers start to get too empty.'

'It's as simple as that?'

Now Thackeray sounded curious.

'More or less. The nice thing about being in my job is that there's always plenty of work when you need it. Haven't you heard, fighting wars is a growth industry?'

Although I was perfectly well aware of what Thackeray was after, he'd have to ask straight out for it. It wasn't something he was at all shy about.

'So you haven't served any prison sentences?'

'No.'

'Does that mean you don't have a police record?'

'I certainly don't have a criminal record, not even for while I was a youngster.'

'But?'

Thackeray was quick to spot the slight hesitation I'd thrown in for him and he wanted to know what it was I was holding back.

'Well, I've never made any secret of what I do for a living,' I told him. 'Besides, I haven't always ended up on the winning side. My name must figure on one or two governmental shit-lists around the world.'

'That happens in business too. Losers never are very popular.'

Sir Keith accompanied his remark with an understanding smile. As he and Thackeray didn't realize I was lying through my teeth, they probably appreciated my honesty.

'If we do decide to employ you,' Thackeray said, 'you may be asked to do things which aren't strictly within the letter of the law.'

'I gathered that when you produced the arsenal from the boot of your car.'

'The possibility doesn't bother you?'

It seemed appropriate to hesitate again before I answered. I felt this would be expected of me.

'There are degrees of illegality,' I said cautiously. 'In my book there's a distinct difference betwen committing a crime and bending the law.'

'I would never allow myself to become involved with anything criminal.' For the first time Sir Keith managed to sound pompous. Until this point he hadn't come on strong, even if there'd been any way he could disguise his wealth. The Rolls and the setting of the country club would have seen to that without the open-necked shirt and slacks which had probably cost as much as my best suit. Some people would maintain Sir Keith had committed a criminal act simply by accumulating the amount of money he had. I wouldn't necessarily agree with them but I refused to believe anybody could become a self-made millionaire without having at least one cupboard with a skeleton inside.

'Look,' I said, allowing a trace of irritation into my voice. 'You're starting to talk in riddles again. Up to date I've answered a hell of a lot of personal questions and neither of you has done more than hint at the job I'm supposed to be applying for. Once I have some inkling of what I'm expected to do, I'll be able to say whether or not I'm prepared to do it.'

It was time for Thackeray and Sir Keith to match significant glances again. On this occasion, however, both their minds were made up. They'd already decided I was the man they wanted, so all they had to determine was who would do the explaining. Even so, Sir Keith didn't exactly burden me with a wealth of detail. All he really told me was that in the next few days Thackeray and I would be expected to escort somebody from the south of France to England. No names, places or dates were mentioned. It didn't take Sir Keith very long to tell me this and once he'd finished I did my best to clear the air with some of the questions I'd be expected to ask.

'Does this person have a valid passport?' I enquired.

'As far as we know, but we won't necessarily be coming through one of the authorized points of entry into this country.'

Sir Keith was leaving this part to Thackeray, and I admired the euphemism for illegal entry.

'Why are bodyguards necessary? Or perhaps I should ask, who is it we'll be trying to avoid?'

'It isn't the police or the Customs. You can rest easy on that score.'

'But I am correct in assuming that somebody will be doing their best to stop us.'

'It is a distinct possibility,' Thackeray conceded.

The whole process was almost as rewarding as trying to squeeze blood out of a stone. After a quarter of an hour or so I had as much of the picture as Thackeray was prepared to give me. Certain parties would have a vested interest in preventing our charge from reaching England and they probably wouldn't be fussy about the methods they used to stop us. If they did interfere with us, Thackeray wouldn't be any fussier about the way he discouraged them. Our absolute priority would be to bring our charge safe and sound to Sir Keith and force would be met with equal force. Although we wouldn't be looking for trouble, we weren't going to allow anything or anybody to get in our way. If it became necessary, I'd be expected to shoot to kill.

'It's the only way to shoot,' I agreed, 'but it does raise an interesting point. Don't the police here and in France have some ridiculous, old-fashioned views about killing people off simply because they're a nuisance?'

'So I've heard.' Thackeray's tone was dry. 'It probably won't come to it but this is one of the risks you'll be recompensed for.'

'Recompense is a word that's always fascinated me,' I prodded.

Now it was Sir Keith's turn.

'The fee for your services will be £10.000,' he said. 'It will be paid into whichever bank you specify on the day you leave for France. If, by any chance, you should fall foul of the law, you'll be paid a further £250 a week until your release can be arranged.'

My low whistle of appreciation was all the answer he needed. I'd have been even more appreciative if I'd been able to convince myself that Sir Keith really was my fairy godmother in drag. Or if I hadn't known that Pawson wouldn't allow me a penny of the money for myself.

SANTA MARIA, ITALY

By now Joseph was almost positive that the woman was alone. It was half an hour since she'd come out of the cottage and she'd displayed no inclination to move. Joseph began another slow sweep of the miniature valley with his binoculars, alert for the slightest movement. There was none. Satisfied on this score, he concentrated on the cottage, straining his eyes to see into the darkened interior. Then, inevitably, the binoculars swung back to the woman herself. Although he was almost a quarter of a mile away in his hiding-place on the hillside, the glasses

were powerful enough to bring everything into fine detail.
Joseph could feel the sharp stab of excitement as he allowed
himself to linger on the bared breasts and the narrow
strip of white cloth across her loins. It required a conscious effort for him to put the binoculars down on the
ground beside him.

His instructions had been explicit. If he did track her
down, he was to do absolutely nothing until help arrived.
He was to find the nearest telephone, contact the Genoa
number he had scrawled down on the scrap of paper in
his pocket and then resume observation. She might be a
woman but he wasn't to underestimate her. On no account must he initiate any independent action. The information she possessed was far too important for any risks to
be taken.

These were the orders and Joseph remembered them
well. He was also fully aware of the consequences of any
disobedience. The people he worked for didn't believe in
second chances. On the other hand, he'd have a mile to
walk before he reached his car, then a five mile drive to
the nearest village. And the woman was alone, he was
sure of it. His disobedience would be overlooked if he
brought her back with him. Her capture would help a lot
of important people to sleep easier in their beds.

Joseph carefully eased himself well back into the
shadow of the trees before he stood up. He'd already
planned his route and he moved both quickly and quietly,
filled with a sense of anticipation. He'd known the bitch
in Kampala, back in the days when the President's infatu-
ation with her had made her a kind of uncrowned queen,
and she'd treated him like dirt. Now the boot would be on
the other foot. She'd be the one to grovel, for all the good
it would do her. He wouldn't be expected to report in until nightfall and this would allow him plenty of time to
discover how well her arrogance had stood up to three
months on the run.

It took him almost twenty minutes to reach the trees directly behind the cottage. Now he needed to be more careful, and Joseph covered the fifty metres of open ground in a crouching run, making sure he kept the building between him and the sleeping woman. Pressed against the rough stone wall, he stopped for a few seconds, listening for any indication that his approach had been observed. Satisfied, he turned his attention to the window on his left, his Walther unholstered and the safety catch off. The interior of the cottage was empty, apart from the sparse furnishings, and Joseph relaxed. It really was going to be as easy as he'd hoped.

Cautiously he moved to the corner of the building and peered round. The woman hadn't moved since he'd been up on the hillside. She was still sprawled on her back on the mattress with her eyes closed. Joseph was close enough to see the regular movement of her breathing and the tiny rivulet of sweat trickling down between her breasts. There was an ugly smile on his face as he stepped out into the open.

'Good afternoon, Princess,' he said, using the honorific as an insult. 'This is an unexpected pleasure.'

When her eyes snapped open, the fear in them was a reward in itself. Joseph was positive there would be many more to follow.

CHAPTER 2

I was lying full length on the floor before my lips had finished unpuckering. Although there was a nice thick carpet to absorb most of the shock, I'd have gone down just as fast even if I'd been landing on bare concrete. When somebody started shooting at me with a rifle, bruises became unimportant. Thackerary's instinct for self-preservation was almost as finely tuned as my own. The only reason he took a fraction of a second longer to reach the safety of the floor was that he'd taken time out to drag Sir Keith down with him.

The two of them were marginally ahead of the second bullet which dislodged another saucer-sized chunk of plaster and wallpaper from the wall behind us. Then there was silence apart from heavy breathing, most of which was coming from me. Long guns terrified me, an attitude which proved how sensible I was. They had accuracy, they had range and they had the kind of muzzle velocity I didn't even want to think about. Worse still, there was very little you could do to combat them unless you happened to have a tank, or a rifle of your own. The fact that there had been no third shot did nothing to encourage me to leap back to my feet. I preferred to stay where I was and examine the pieces of glass from the window which were littering the carpet.

'Tell me,' I said. 'This isn't another of your little initiative tests, is it?'

'It isn't.' I was irrationally pleased to detect the faintest tremor in Thackeray's voice. 'This definitely wasn't scripted.'

We settled down to another brief silence while I wondered what type of rifle was being used. I couldn't help remembering that some of them were perfectly capable of shooting right through walls. It was left to Sir Keith to come up with a constructive suggestion.

'Wouldn't we be safer somewhere else?' he said. 'There aren't any windows in the corridor.'

'You're probably right.'

I knew why Thackeray wasn't sounding particularly enthusiastic. However much he fancied the bit about a windowless corridor, he didn't like the idea of exposing himself to the sniper. This was precisely what we'd have to do to reach the door on the far side of the room.

'We certainly can't stay here all day,' I agreed. 'I'll go first if you like.'

Although I did my best to sound brave and heroic, I doubted whether I was fooling Thackeray for a moment. The first crossing should come as a big surprise to our sniper. By the second and third he should be ready. The only real gamble I'd be taking would be on how fast I could open the door.

The route I selected was an intricate one, specifically designed to keep me under the cover afforded by the tables for as long as possible. For the last stretch there was nothing except carpet and I paused for a second or two before attempting it, briefly toying with the idea of dragging one of the tables along with me. Unfortunately, they were so flimsy that any sense of security would be entirely illusory. About all a table would do for me was slow me down.

The only answer was to go hard and fast and pray that the door didn't stick. I took the time for a brief mental rehearsal, then I was off, marvelling at the speed I derived from fear-induced adrenalin. I fitted in four long strides, wrenched open the door and dived into the corridor with an impetus which had me bouncing off the far wall as I rolled to safety. Only then could I register the fact that no further shot had been fired.

'OK, Philis?' Thackeray called.

'I'm fine. You'd better come next, Sir Keith. Choose your own time, but make it fast when you decide to try.'

I didn't bother to add that it was impossible to outpace rifle bullets, no matter how fast you ran. I was too busy wondering exactly what kind of a mess Pawson had pitch-forked me into this time.

It was almost five minutes before all three of us were cowering safely in the corridor. There had been no further shots and now was the time to think constructively

again. At least, this was what Thackeray thought he was
doing.

'You stay here with Sir Keith, Philis,' he said. 'I'm going to make a try for my car.'

'You're going for the weapons?'

Thackeray nodded.

'Too right I am. We're going to need some form of protection if that bastard out there decides to come in after
us.'

'He won't.' I was speaking with a conviction I didn't entirely feel. 'Our friend with the rifle should be long gone
by now.'

This was a sure way of holding everybody's attention.
Although the events of the last few minutes had made Sir
Keith start to look his age, my few words of comfort
snapped his brain back into gear again. He desperately
wanted my assessment of the situation to be correct.

'What makes you think that?' he asked.

'There are several things,' I told him. 'For a start, he
was hiding in the copse of trees at the top of the hill. He
couldn't possibly have missed with a rifle if he'd seriously
intended to kill anybody. I'd guess he was putting a warning shot or two across our bows to frighten us. Speaking
for myself, I'd say he was one hundred per cent
successful.'

'Go on, Philis.'

Thackeray wasn't disagreeing with me. He simply
wanted to hear the rest of my reasoning.

'OK. Let's assume for a moment that the gunman really is
the world's worst marksman. This wouldn't have stopped
him from taking a few more potshots at us when we tried
for the door. All of us must have been in clear view.'

'He might not have seen us,' Sir Keith pointed out. 'He
could have been moving closer to the clubhouse at the
time.'

'That is a possibility,' I conceded, 'but it presupposes

he's a complete idiot as well. He already had us pinned down. He knew one of us would have to make a move sooner or later, so there was no reason for him to change his position. I'd say he made a beeline for the perimeter wall as soon as he'd put a couple of bullets over our heads.'

Now the initial panic had died down, I could see both the others tended to agree with me. However, one crucial question remained to be answered. Thackeray was the man to phrase it for us.

'It's a fine theory,' he said slowly. 'How do we find out whether it's correct or not?'

'There's no need to test it.' I'd had my reply ready. 'All we have to do is telephone the police and sit tight.'

Sir Keith's head started shaking slightly before Thackeray's. This illustrated one of several points which had been intriguing me. When law-abiding citizens are assaulted with deadly weapons, their first thought is usually to contact the lads in blue. Until I'd mentioned the obvious, neither Thackeray nor Sir Keith had spared a glance for the telephone a few feet down the hallway from us.

'I'd prefer that to be our very last resort,' Sir Keith told me. 'In view of what we were discussing, it would be unwise for the three of us to attract the attention of the authorities. It could cause some awkward questions.'

'Fair enough.' My shrug was supposed to indicate that this was no more than I'd expected. 'In that case, I suggest you stay here with Mr Thackeray. I'll go outside and see what I can find.'

Nobody tried to dissuade me. As I headed for the main entrance, I hoped I'd added a bit more lustre to the hero image I was trying to project. It might be a sham but it should help to convince my new employers that they'd picked the right man for the job.

Although my mouth was a trifle dry when I stepped out

into the open, I'd never been the foolhardy type and I wasn't about to make any changes now. I was almost convinced that my predictions about the gunman's actions were right but I wasn't gambling on this alone. If somebody had come to the country club with murder in his heart, he hadn't been gunning for anybody called Philis. I was strictly an optional extra and this was why I made a big production out of keeping both hands in clear view. If the gunman was still around, I wanted him to know how harmless I was.

After I'd covered the first few yards and no bullets had ripped through my flesh, I began to relax. It was only about a three-minute walk to the copse and once I was in the trees it didn't take me very long to discover the firing point. The small hollow the sniper had made himself in the undergrowth was impossible to miss, although the shell casings had been neatly tidied up. I did look under the odd bush or two but there was no sign of them anywhere.

It was fairly easy to see where the gunman had gone after he'd fired his second shot, and I followed his trail until I reached the far side of the copse, coming out of the trees into the rough adjoining one of the fairways of the golf course. It was pointless to go any further. By now the sniper would be halfway back to London or wherever his base was. It seemed a far better idea to return to the clubhouse and try Thackeray and Sir Keith with a few more questions.

I'd always suspected that sitting behind the wheel of a Rolls must be one of life's more satisfying experiences, a kind of ego trip on wheels. Now I had the chance to find out, the character on the motorbike was doing his level best to spoil it for me.

Questioning Thackeray and Sir Keith definitely hadn't afforded me any satisfaction. In fact, it had been almost as frustrating as I'd expected it to be. Although both of them had conceded that the shooting had probably been connected with the job they were hiring me to do, this was the most they were prepared to tell me and I hadn't pushed too hard. As Thackeray had been quick to point out, they wouldn't have been paying me so much if there hadn't been considerable risks involved.

I'd inherited the Corniche after I'd been successfully sidetracked into completing the financial arrangements. Thackeray hadn't wanted Sir Keith to travel home alone. Furthermore, he'd reasoned that if there was going to be any further trouble his Porsche would be more of an asset than the Rolls. Rather than leave the Corniche to add distinction to the car park, Sir Keith had asked me to drive it back to London for him and I hadn't raised any objections. In fact, I'd been quite enjoying the envious glances from the other road-users until the motorbike had slotted in behind me.

The tag had first materialized in the driving mirror within a quarter of a mile of the country club and he hadn't made any attempt to conceal himself. Perhaps he had the sense to realize that for someone his size and colour, on a bright red Honda, being inconspicuous was an impossibility. He was enormous, completely dwarfing the machine he was riding, and he was the blackest man I'd ever seen. Although it would have been simple enough to lose him, this wasn't one of my priorities — I'd satisfied myself there was nowhere on the Honda he could possibly hide a rifle. He'd aroused my curiosity and I wanted to discover just how blatant he was prepared to be.

When the Corniche swept majestically into the layby, the motorcyclist followed, halting fifty yards behind where I'd parked. For a minute or two I smoked a Senior Service and watched him in the mirror. The motorcyclist had lit a cigarette of his own and was watching me watch him. This wasn't getting us anywhere so, hoping for more meaningful communication, I eased myself out of the driving seat. For the first twenty yards he puffed at his cigarette and watched my advance. Then he abruptly kick-started the Honda into life, did a U-turn and headed slowly back towards the road, looking at me over his shoulder.

I was too old to run unless it was absolutely necessary and shouting was too undignified for the driver of a Rolls so I stopped. So did the motorcyclist. When I started towards him again, he moved a little closer to the road. This was when I decided meaningful communication was a hell of a sight more trouble than it was worth.

We did the rest of the journey into central London in convoy. As soon as I'd parked the Corniche in the private car park Sir Keith had specified, I headed for the nearest telephone. There was no answer at the number Thackeray had given me, but I had better luck with SR(2) headquarters.

'I'm being followed by a large black man,' I explained.

'Lucky old you,' Patterson simpered. 'It must be the way you swing your hips.'

I wouldn't have laughed even if I'd been particularly amused. The theory was that there must be some strange virus which afflicted duty officers, convincing them all they were comedians. Unless an emergency prefix was used, they all felt compelled to push some tired, old wisecrack and I'd never have forgiven myself if I'd given Patterson any encouragement.

Once he'd finished chortling at his own wit, I gave him a description and waited while he flicked through the current hot list. Although I wasn't particularly surprised to discover there was no mention of giant Africans on Hondas, this was something I'd had to check. I bravely suffered through Patterson's farewell banana joke, then went back outside to where my escort was patiently waiting. There still wasn't any reason to ditch him so I hailed a taxi and left him to get on with his thing. He wasn't any less conspicuous in the London traffic than he had been on the open road. It took the taxi-driver all of a minute to spot him.

'Hey,' he said. 'We're being followed.'

'You must be imagining things.'

'I'm not.' The driver was taking himself very seriously. 'There's a bloody great African on a motorbike behind us. He's been there ever since I picked you up.'

As denials weren't any good, I fobbed the driver off with a singularly unconvincing explanation and an outsize tip at the end of the journey. The man on the Honda seemed totally oblivious to any attention he might be attracting and his surveillance of my flat was every bit as discreet as it had been on the road. When I looked out of the window, he was directly across the street, straddling his motorbike and staring unblinkingly back at me. I tried him with a friendly wave and he completely ignored it. However, after a couple of unrewarding minutes he carefully propped the Honda up on its stand and set off along the street.

I watched him until he'd rounded the corner, then I wandered into the kitchen to prepare myself a snack. It ended up as a *cordon gris* collation of fried eggs, bacon and tomatoes and by the time I'd tastefully slopped it on to a plate, my shadow had been reunited with his motorbike. I munched away at the table by the window and kept an eye on him. He wasn't doing much except stare back at me. It wasn't until I was forking the last mouthful into my mouth that there was a development.

The driver of the battered green Mini was every bit as black as the motorcyclist and about three sizes smaller, a chubby little man dressed in an immaculate pinstriped suit. There was a brief conference by the Honda, then the two of them started across the road. I barely had time to dump my plate and cutlery in the sink before the doorbell rang.

'I'm Alfred Mukwaya,' the little man announced. 'May I come in?'

He pressed an ornate business card into my hand before slipping past me into the flat. Rather than be trampled underfoot, I stepped back smartly before his companion followed him in. According to the card, Mr Mukwaya was an engineering consultant and dealer in African objets d'art. This didn't strike me as the most likely of combinations.

'I also contribute occasional articles to the *Taifa Empya* and the *Argus*,' he told me. By now Mukwaya was comfortably settled in an armchair with his friend standing sentry duty behind him. 'They are leading Ugandan newspapers.'

'Bully for you,' I said. 'What about Man Mountain here? Does he do anything apart from following me?'

Mr Mukwaya laughed merrily. He really was a jolly little fellow.

'We were interested in you,' he explained. 'I'm afraid Sam doesn't speak English very well.'

'Come to that, he's not too hot on a motorbike. He either ought to have his legs shortened or buy himself a bigger machine.'

This was an excuse for Mr Mukwaya to laugh again.

'I see you have the famous British sense of humour, Mr Philis. Unfortunately, I want to talk to you about a very serious matter. You were keeping bad company this afternoon.'

'I was?'

The abrupt change of tack had me temporarily off balance.

'Most definitely. Sir Keith Tenby and Mr Thackeray are not very nice people.'

'That's your opinion. They struck me as being most pleasant.'

'You must never be deceived by first appearances, Mr

Philis.' Now Mukwaya was looking serious. 'For example, I'm small and I laugh and smile a lot. This convinces a lot of people that I'm innocuous, but they're mistaken. I make a very dangerous enemy. Very dangerous indeed.'

Although the threat should have been ridiculous coming from somebody his height and build, Mukwaya had spoken with quiet conviction. Besides, he had the massive bulk of Sam looming behind him to add weight to his words.

'You're talking as though we're already enemies.'

'We may well be. Did Sir Keith offer you employment?'

'I don't really see how that's any of your business.'

Even without his bodyguard, Mukwaya would no longer have impressed me as being at all innocuous. Despite the pinstripe suit, the meticulous English and the obvious intelligence, the veneer of Western civilization was only as deep as he wanted it to be. Behind the shield of his slightly hooded eyes, I suspected that Mukwaya retained all the patterns of tribal behaviour. 'Primitive' was a word he'd rightly have found offensive but I'd always been wary of modes of behaviour I didn't understand. I doubted very much whether Mukwaya placed as much value on human life as I'd have liked him to.

'I think you have answered my question, Mr Philis,' he was saying. 'There would be no necessity for you to prevaricate unless Sir Keith had made you an offer of some description.'

He stopped for a moment to see whether I had any comment to make. When I declined his unspoken invitation, he continued.

'Under the present circumstances,' he said, 'it's difficult to see how a conflict of interests can be avoided. Sir Keith Tenby is no friend of the Ugandan people and any form of association with him would inevitably taint you. Unless, of course . . .'

Mukwaya had allowed his voice to tail away. He should

have held up a cue-card to announce that this was a significant pause.

'Unless?' I prompted.

'I haven't had an opportunity to check you thoroughly, Mr Philis,' he went on, 'but I have learned a little. In my part of the world the word "mercenary" has most unpleasant connotations. We think of mercenaries as killers for hire, men who subordinate human suffering to their own greed. However, I'm enough of a realist to appreciate that there are occasions when they have their uses. There are times when their very lack of idealism becomes a positive asset. As money is the only thing they honour and respect, there are no problems about deciding the best way to approach them.'

He'd spoken with icy contempt and he was equally contemptuous when he pulled the bulky envelope from his jacket pocket. Rather than hand it to me, he tossed the envelope on to the coffee table in front of him.

'What's that?' I asked.

'Can't you guess, Mr Philis? Weren't you listening to what I was saying? I'm paying tribute to your own particular god. There is one thousand pounds inside the envelope. You're at perfect liberty to check if you so desire.'

I made no move to touch the envelope. Playing coy was pointless, but I didn't want to make it too easy for the Ugandan.

'What do I have to do to earn it?' I asked. 'Agree not to work for Sir Keith?'

'Far from it.' Mukwaya had reverted to his jolly self and was laughing. 'Do everything Sir Keith asks of you. Be a conscientious employee and gain his confidence. Learn what you can of his intentions, then pass the information on to me. That's what I'm paying you for.'

I started to speak, but Mukwaya held up a hand to stop me. Although he was still smiling broadly, I didn't find his mood at all infectious.

'Don't commit yourself immediately,' he told me. 'Take twenty-four hours to think over my proposition. You can always contact me at the telephone number on my business card.'

He rose to his feet to deliver the punch line.

'Just try to remember one thing, Mr Philis. I'm an excellent marksman and it would have been a simple matter to put a bullet through your head this afternoon. I chose not to, but it would take very little to persuade me to change my mind.'

He left the envelope on the table when he went and I didn't try to force him to take it back. As far as Mukwaya was concerned, the contract had been concluded. It was blood money, and I owned the blood which was at stake.

SANTA MARIA, ITALY

'Hello, Princess,' the voice said. 'This is an unexpected pleasure.'

Kuldip was half-asleep in the warm sun and the shock was total. For one long, awful moment it was as though time stood still, she was literally paralysed with fear. Although she'd accepted the risks when she'd first decided to capitalize on what she knew and there had never been any doubt in her mind about what would happen if she was caught, Kuldip hadn't really expected it to come to this. She'd known they were getting close — this was why she'd prepared her escape route — but she'd thought she had at least another week. Now she knew better.

When she managed to force her eyes open, Kuldip recognized Joseph immediately. She didn't know his name, of course, because there had never been any form of social contact. He'd been one of the SRB thugs, impossible to forget with the pock-marks on both cheeks. Although they'd never actually spoken, Kuldip had been aware of him, the same way she was always aware of the men who desired her. She'd known he was mentally stripping her and, far from insulting her, she'd found the knowledge vaguely exciting. It had given her a sense of power. Now, Kuldip thought, he won't have to rely on his imagination any longer. He's seen just about all there is to see of me.

Already, within a second of Joseph having spoken, the initial shock had died away. Although she still looked frightened, Kuldip was using her apparent fear as a weapon while she sought a way out.

'Up on your feet, bitch,' Joseph said. 'Let's go into the house.'

Kuldip made herself move slowly and reluctantly, doing her best to give the impression of being cowed and beaten. The gun in his hand was an irrelevance, she'd decided. She was far too valuable to shoot. The important thing was that the man appeared to be on his own. If he was, there weren't going to be any problems. While she didn't approve of casting pearls in front of swine, every rule had to have its exception.

'Why don't you put the gun away?' Kuldip suggested. 'We both know you're not going to use it.'

'I wouldn't be so sure if I was you.'

Joseph failed to muster a great deal of conviction. Somewhere between the mattress and the interior of the cottage he'd lost the initiative. Far from being frightened, all the woman's old confidence and arrogance had returned.

'Be realistic,' she said. 'Your instructions are to take me back alive. Of course,' she added, 'if you're as sensible as I think you are, you won't want to take me back at all.'

'What do you mean?'

It took a conscious effort for Joseph to speak, and his
voice sounded thick. The bitch was deliberately flaunting
herself in front of him, perfectly well aware of the effect
she had. Joseph had desired her from the moment he'd
first set eyes on her but until now scenes like this had had
to be fabricated in his imagination.

'You're alone,' Kuldip pointed out. 'Does anybody else
know you're here?'

'No. I haven't had time to report in yet.'

By now Joseph had realized what she was trying to do
and he was actively encouraging her. Although he wasn't
nearly as big a fool as she seemed to think, he was quite
content to play her game while it suited him. When she'd
given him what he'd have taken anyway, Joseph would let
her know she hadn't deceived him for a moment. It
should make her humiliation complete.

'Exactly,' Kuldip continued, seemingly unaware of
what was going on in the man's mind. 'You're free to do
what you want. You certainly don't owe the bastards who
sent you after me any favours. They're the reason you had
to leave Uganda.'

'That's true, I suppose.'

'Of course it is.' Kuldip was really pushing now. 'And
what do they pay you? A mere pittance, I bet. You'd find
I was far more generous.'

'You mean you have money? Here in the house?'

Kuldip laughed at Joseph's eagerness, knowing she had
him now.'

'No, not here,' she told him, 'but don't worry. You'll be
well paid. Besides, there's more to a partnership than
mere cash.'

As she spoke, Kuldip hooked her thumbs under the
elastic of her bikini briefs and slid them down over her
thighs.

Joseph had all the subtlety of a bull elephant in season.

He'd no time for either foreplay or finesse and he seemed oblivious to the way he was crushing her as he pounded frantically away. At least, Kuldip thought, he's finally put the bloody gun down. He would have taken her anyway, whether she'd been willing or not, and she preferred so suffer his attentions without a gun held to her head.

'Oh, Christ,' she moaned, moving her hips against him. 'That's so good.'

Joseph simply grunted and ploughed on, intent on his own pleasure. Men are such fools, Kuldip decided as she slid the knife from beneath the pillow. It's as though an erection drains all the blood from their brains.

'Oh, yes,' she moaned again, running the fingers of her left hand down Joseph's spine. 'That's wonderful.'

CHAPTER 3

The newspaper headline didn't exactly jump off the page and hit me in the eye, but it did stop me chomping my cornflakes for a second or two. After I'd read through the article which went with the headline I abandoned the cornflakes altogether, leaving the unfinished bowl on the kitchen table while I went to look out of the living-room window. Although there were no obviously suspicious characters lurking in the street below, this didn't necessarily mean a great deal. Not everybody had to make themselves as conspicuous as Sam.

When I telephoned in, Pawson hadn't yet reached SR(2) headquarters. Nor was he at home, so I had myself patched through to the radio-telephone in his car. It was a procedure I considered justified by the urgency of my predicament.

'What's happened?'

Pawson didn't sound as though he welcomed the intrusion.

'Didn't you receive my report?'

'I saw it, yes.'

'In that case you can't have read further than the sports section of *The Times* before you left home. It seems that Mukwaya is dead.'

'Dead?' Some of my urgency was beginning to communicate itself to Pawson. 'How did it happen?'

'According to the newspapers he was the innocent victim of a bomb outrage. In the light of what we know, I find that most unlikely.'

For a few seconds the static on the line was all I had to listen to. It went without saying that Pawson knew a hell of a sight more than I did. This meant it took him a little bit longer to fit the pieces together.

'I'll contact the police and the bomb squad immediately,' he decided. 'That doesn't solve our major problem, though. Do you want me to arrange you alternative accommodation until the situation has stabilized?'

'Not yet,' I told him. 'I'd rather take my chances here for the time being. Any attempt to go into hiding is going to look like an admission of guilt.'

'You're probably right, Philis,' Pawson conceded, 'but I don't want you taking any unnecessary risks. It would be pointless to get yourself killed at this stage of the operation.'

I wasn't entirely happy with the way Pawson had phrased himself. I'd no intention of getting myself killed at any stage of any operation.

'What worries me most at the moment,' I said, 'is how I'm going to handle Thackeray. If I come on too strong, I'm likely to be out of a job. On the other hand, this isn't something he'd expect me to ignore.'

There was another brief session of static while Pawson considered my dilemma.

'You'll have to play it by ear,' he contributed helpfully. 'Let me know how it goes, though. I'll be available to see you when you manage to make headquarters.'

It seemed that this was going to be all the help I was likely to receive so I left Pawson to enjoy the rest of his drive in peace and made my second telephone call of the morning. Thackeray evidently hadn't read the newspapers either, and I didn't bother with details. All I told him was that I had to see him immediately. I also warned him to make sure he wasn't followed on the way to our rendezvous. Then I hung up before Thackeray had an opportunity to ask me any questions.

Another look out of the window confirmed my worst fears. The yellow Cavalier which was parked a hundred yards down the street had arrived since I'd last checked and I couldn't think of too many reasons why the driver should still be sitting in the car. Anywhere else and he might have been admiring the scenic beauties, but these were a bit thin on the ground in Shepherds Bush. Although the driver was sitting in shadow and it was impossible to be absolutely positive, he looked like another African and I was rapidly developing racist tendencies. For the moment, black was bloody dangerous.

Fortunately nobody was covering the back of the building and I travelled the first mile on foot before I grabbed a taxi, practising some of the routines Garbo should have learned to help her to be alone. At the other end, I had the taxi-driver drop me a quarter of a mile from the site of the rendezvous and did a general sweep of the area. While this didn't really prove anything, it did seem as though Thackeray had been as careful as I'd warned him to be.

There were hardly any customers in the cafe and Thackeray had selected a table in the corner where he could watch the door. I slapped the newspaper down in front of him, neatly folded so he couldn't possibly miss

what he was supposed to see, then I went up to the
counter. By the time I was back with a muddy-looking
cup of coffee, he'd finished reading the article.

'Well?' I demanded, slipping into the seat opposite
him.

'What am I supposed to say? Apparently you've pre-
judged us already.'

Thackeray seemed genuinely shaken by the news but
this could be misleading. I didn't know him well enough
to be sure of how good an actor he was.

'Shouldn't I have done?' I asked. Cynicism had always
come easily to me. 'You have to admit it's one hell of a
coincidence. I telephone to tell you about Mukwaya's
courtesy call and a few hours later his body is splattered
all over Knightsbridge. I don't want any part of murder.'

'It's not being offered to you.' Thackeray's sincerity
came across well. 'Neither I nor Sir Keith had anything to
do with Mukwaya's death.'

'You'll have to do better than that. Denials come
cheap.'

'OK.' Now the initial shock had worn off, Thackeray
was behaving as though he had full command of himself
and the situation. 'Perhaps I can convince you we didn't
have any reason to consider Mukwaya a threat. I did some
checking after you contacted me yesterday evening and I
didn't learn anything to worry me. Mukwaya occasionally
represented the Ugandan government in an unofficial
capacity, low-grade intelligence work and the like. His
interest in what Sir Keith and I are doing was only
peripheral.'

'That wasn't the way it struck me. He appeared to be
taking a very keen interest in what you're doing. A thousand pounds isn't exactly chickenfeed.'

This made Thackeray laugh.

'You'd be amazed at how many official and private
bodies are poking their noses into Sir Keith's affairs at any

given time. That's basically why he employs me. Financial espionage is an even bigger growth industry than fighting wars. What Mukwaya offered you really is chickenfeed compared to what certain parties would be prepared to pay for details of some of Sir Keith's operations.'

'Mukwaya was no financier.' I couldn't allow myself to be won over too easily. 'He referred to you two as enemies of Uganda.'

'He would have done.' Thackeray's amused, rather condescending smile seemed completely natural. 'By his lights we were. Sir Keith has extensive holdings in Africa, some of them in Uganda. His crime was to make money out of them while Amin was in power. In Kampala nowadays you only need to have shaken hands with Amin to automatically qualify as an enemy of the state.'

'And that's all there is to it?'

'You have my word on it. Mukwaya was no more than a nuisance. In any case, even if he had posed a threat, we wouldn't have resorted to violence. That isn't the way Sir Keith does business.'

'Of course not. I realized he was a pacifist the moment I saw those guns in the boot of your car.'

'There's a considerable difference between cold-blooded murder and being prepared to protect yourself.' Thackeray was being very patient. 'I'd have thought you would have appreciated the distinction better than most, Philis. What's more, the threat we're hiring you to guard against is entirely criminal in origin. It has nothing at all to do with the present government of Uganda.'

Thackeray paused to allow me an opportunity to comment. Although I'd made a mental note of his emphasis on 'the present government' and I certainly wasn't buying everything he'd told me, it was time to stop playing the reluctant virgin.

'However,' Thackeray continued, spelling out the alter-

natives for me, 'if you do still have any doubts, you're at
perfect liberty to back out of the agreement we reached
yesterday. We'd recompense you for the time and inconvenience and, in return, we'd naturally expect you to
keep quiet about the matters we discussed.'

Although Thackeray was fairly confident about my
response, he'd have been even more confident if he'd
realized that I didn't have any alternatives at all. Unless
Pawson said otherwise, I was stuck with the job whether I
wanted it or not.

Before I left Thackeray we had one other matter to discuss. I told him about the Cavalier parked outside my flat
and why I thought it was there. Mukwaya's associates
wouldn't believe in coincidences either. They were going
to add two and two together to make five, pinpointing me
as the man most likely to have sent Mukwaya a bomb. As
I said, Thackeray and Sir Keith would almost inevitably
attract the same kind of attention until the real killers
were found.

Thackeray's immediate reaction was the same as
Pawson's, a suggestion that I ought to go undercover until
it was time to leave for France. My response also stayed
the same. Innocent men didn't need to hide. The alternative course of action I proposed didn't receive a particularly enthusiastic reception.

'You're crazy, Philis,' Thackeray told me. 'You'll be
handing yourself to them on a plate.'

'Maybe,' I conceded, 'but at least it should help to clear
the air. It can't possibly be construed as the action of a
guilty man.'

'No,' Thackeray agreed. 'More like a madman. What's
the point of it?'

'You suggested it yourself when I first told you about
Mukwaya last night. The information I feed them doesn't
necessarily have to be one hundred per cent accurate and

so long as I maintain some form of contact we'll have an idea of what Mukwaya's friends are doing. With any luck it gets me off the hook as well. They're not going to kill me while they think I'm useful.'

Although Thackeray still wasn't impressed with my logic, he didn't make any more attempts to dissuade me. As I'd said, what I was doing might pay dividends for him. If it didn't and things turned sour, he'd always be able to hire himself another mercenary.

The easiest way to establish contact would have been by telephone. Unfortunately, the voice which answered when I tried the number Mukwaya had given me had 'policeman' stamped all over it. I hung up while I was still being asked who I was. The other approach was more direct but it entailed considerably more risk. The Cavalier was still where I'd last seen it and I went towards it from behind, keeping on the driver's blind side. As I'd suspected, he was another African and I immediately classified him as a thug. Even after I'd tapped on the window he didn't recognize me.

'My name is Philis,' I told him. 'Who am I supposed to report to now Mukwaya is dead?'

For a second nothing registered on the African's face. A long knife-scar curved down his cheek from above one eyebrow and there was something in his yellowish blood-flecked eyes which warned me I'd underrated him. The man wasn't simply a thug. He was a killer.

'Get in,' he said at last, speaking in atrocious English. 'I'll take you to him.'

I did as he'd said and we sat in silence during the short drive into Notting Hill. Our destination was about a quarter of a mile from the Tube station, a flat in a building which seemed semi-derelict. The man inside was no great improvement on the driver. He didn't have a knife-scar but that was about all. Before he said anything to me he conducted a brief conversation with the man

from the Cavalier, both of them talking in what I assumed
was a Ugandan dialect. It hadn't escaped my notice that
my former driver had stationed himself behind me where
he effectively barred the only exit.

'Well, Mr Philis?' The second man's English was only
marginally better than that of his companion. 'What do
you want?'

I shrugged. I was beginning to agree with Thackeray.
This had all the hallmarks of a major mistake.

'I was hoping to clear the air,' I said. 'I wanted you to
know that I didn't have anything to do with Mukwaya's
death.'

'We know that already.'

I didn't like his smile any more than I liked having
somebody standing behind me.

'You do?'

'Of course. After all, we were the ones who planted the
bomb.'

This was the moment when I realized just how major
my mistake had been. I knew it even before the driver of
the Cavalier prodded a gun into my back.

Despite the lump on the back of my head, there had been
nothing wrong with my thinking. Certain situations
demanded certain responses and my immediate predicament had been a very basic one. Two men, one gun, a
closed room and the need to get out. This was all there
was to it. Training plus experience plus observation had
all combined to suggest that the time to get out was immediately. People had pointed guns at me before and,
provided they didn't pull the trigger, this didn't worry me
nearly as much as my Ugandan friends probably thought.
The gun was a deterrent, nothing more, and it wasn't going to deter me from doing what was necessary to safe-
guard my priceless skin.

Unfortunately, there were sometimes disadvantages to

a professional approach. It didn't always take account of the unpredictability of amateur sadists. When I made my decision, I had the situation under control. It was simply a matter of re-checking distances before I triggered off the pre-programmed routine which would leave me with the gun and the enemy forces in disarray. When the driver of the Cavalier decided to hit me just for the hell of it, everything fell apart because this hadn't been included in my pre-programming. The gun made solid contact with the back of my head, I was down on my knees on the threadbare carpet and before my brains had a chance to unscramble themselves I was being securely strapped to a chair. Obviously the Ugandans were professionals of a kind too, with their own established routines.

There was a limit to the length of time I could sit with my eyes closed and my head slumped forward on my chest. Ugandan dialects hadn't been included on my syllabus at school so I wasn't gaining much by eavesdropping on the two men's conversation and I didn't need the time to decide what I intended to do next. This was going to be decided for me by my captors.

My carefully acted return to consciousness didn't spark any immediate reaction apart from an incurious glance. The two men simply continued with their unintelligible conversation as if I wasn't there. It occurred to me that they might have conducted the odd interrogation before. Certainly their nonchalance indicated some familiarity with the role. It also occurred to me that I ought to start yelling my head off in the hope of alerting any Good Samaritans there might be in the vicinity. Then I thought of all the ways the Ugandans might stop me yelling and filed the idea away as a last resort. For the time being it was also my only resort. My stock of bright ideas had temporarily exhausted itself, round about the time the gun had made contact with the back of my head.

After a couple of minutes, the man who had been in

the room when I arrived picked up his chair and brought
it across to sit close beside me. He allowed one large hand
to drop casually on to the top of my thigh. I very much
doubted whether the threat implicit in the gesture was
sexual in nature.

'Tell me all about yourself, Mr Philis,' he suggested.

I told him. At least, I told him the authorized version
according to Pawson, the one which featured me as an in-
trepid mercenary. Although I spun it out for as long as
possible, I had to finish the fairy tale eventually. This was
the cue for the serious questioning to begin.

'Why did Mukwaya come to see you yesterday evening?'
the driver asked.

He'd also moved his chair across to sit beside me. We
made a cosy little group.

'He wanted information from me, information I didn't
have.'

'What kind of information?'

Both men were very patient with me. This was an attitude which would persist just so long as I answered all
their questions promptly and satisfactorily. It gave me an
incentive to go through it all. There was no particular
reason to lie and the longer I talked, the longer I'd have to
dream up something which might keep me alive and intact once they'd finished with me. I already knew that the
straps holding me to the chair were going to stay in place
until somebody felt like releasing me.

Once I'd finished with the events of the previous day,
they brought me forward in time. Why had I wanted to
contact Mukwaya's associates? Where had I gone to
before I approached the driver of the Cavalier? Whom
had I spoken to? While I was satisfying their curiosity, I
hoped against hope that I'd misjudged them, that their
plans for my future were radically different from what I
envisaged. Perhaps they really would untie me, pat me on
the head and apologize for inconveniencing me. After all,

the hero always won out in the books I read.

To begin with, though, they lapsed into another of the conversations I wished I understood. All I could do was sit where I was and feel utterly helpless. I'd told them everything I was prepared to and we'd reached the point of no return. Either they let me go or I'd have to start yelling my head off. My alternatives didn't stretch any further than this.

It didn't take the two of them long to reach their decision. I could tell which way it would go from the big, friendly smile on the face of the man to my right. His hand hadn't moved from my thigh and now he gave it an affectionate squeeze. I didn't find the gesture any more comforting than his smile.

'Now,' he said, 'we find out what you forgot to mention.'

This should have been when I started shouting but I knew it wouldn't work. The second man had already switched on the transistor radio on the table beside him, turning the volume control full on. My captors obviously expected me to yell and scream, and this was a contingency they were prepared to cope with.

NOTTING HILL, LONDON

'Who's that with Kibedi?' Kibunka asked.

'I don't know for sure,' Kironde answered. 'He looks like the mercenary Mukwaya visited yesterday.'

The two of them were sitting in their Cortina. Neither of them spoke again until they had watched the Englishman and the ex-SRB man inside the building.

'We must have been wrong. It looks as though the mercenary did have something to do with the bombing after all.'

'I doubt it.'

Kironde had never believed in wasting words.

'Why else would he be here unless he was working with them?'

'There could be several reasons. Perhaps Kibedi and Semakula want to know what he was discussing with Alfred yesterday.'

'You mean they've tricked him into coming here?'

'It's a possibility.'

'If you're right, hadn't we better move in now?'

'Why? I don't play nursemaid to soldiers of fortune.'

There were times when Kibunka didn't fully understand his friend, and this was one of them. It took him a few seconds to think of the right words to use.

'Haven't Semakula and his kind caused enough suffering?' he said. 'Isn't that supposed to be the reason we're here in London?'

Kironde rarely smiled but when he did it was as though his whole face had lit up.

'You're right, as usual.' As he spoke Kironde bent to pick up the sawn-off shotgun which was lying between the two front seats. 'You know what to do.'

Then Kironde was gone, striding across the road with the shotgun concealed beneath his coat. Kibunka was glad he'd been left in charge of the men outside the building. Unlike his friend, he no longer had any stomach for the killing.

CHAPTER 4

Not everybody thought to carry their own portable torture kit around with them but the Ugandans must have been Boy Scouts at heart because they'd come prepared. The crocodile clips and transformer were old hat, crude, brutal and unsophisticated. Unfortunately, this wasn't going to make them any less painful, especially if the clips were attached where I thought they were going to be. What worried me most, though, was my total helplessness. I couldn't move from the chair and I didn't think I could talk myself free. Even if I revealed who I really worked for, something I had every intention of doing before they started passing high voltages through my tackle, I'd still only be delaying the inevitable. They'd still give me the shock treatment, just to make sure there wasn't anything else I'd neglected to tell them. And when they'd finished hurting me, they'd still decide they'd be safer with me dead.

The possibility of outside intervention hadn't occurred to me, except as wishful thinking, and I was as surprised as anybody when the door burst inwards, crashing back against the wall. Kironde didn't tell me his name until later but at the time I couldn't have cared less. He'd only needed the one kick to destroy the lock and he was equally decisive once the door was open. The other two Ugandans seemed rooted to the spot, mesmerized by the man standing in the doorway who was casually holding a sawn-off shotgun in one hand. Both of them were dead before they could move.

At least, one was dead and the other was dying, because the driver of the Cavalier was still twitching as his life's blood pumped out on to the carpet. Kironde didn't allow him to twitch for long, only for the length of time it took him to reload the shotgun. Then he walked across to him and blew his head off where he lay.

'Scum,' he said to nobody in particular. 'The world will be a better place without them.'

I could hear what he said because he'd turned off the radio before he started to go through the dead men's pockets. From there he proceeded to suitcases, drawers and wardrobes. Nothing he found there appeared to

interest him any more than I did because so far he'd hardly
looked at me. It was only after he'd finished his fruitless
search and checked at the door to make sure there was no
untoward activity outside that he condescended to talk to
me.

'Do you know who I am?' he enquired.

'You're a friend of Mr Mukwaya's,' I hazarded.

It didn't require a Sherlock Holmes to make the con-
nection. He hadn't just been kicking doors open at random.

'That is correct. My name is Kironde. You're the
mercenary called Philis unless I'm very much mistaken.'

'You're not,' I told him. 'It's very nice meeting you and
I'm grateful for what you've done, but hadn't we better
get the hell out of here. Otherwise the police are going to
want to know who gave you your licence to kill.'

'There's no rush.' Kironde was sounding as casual as
ever. 'I'll have plenty of warning before we're disturbed.'

He'd settled one buttock on the edge of the table and
he was looking down at me as though he wasn't quite sure
what to do with me. Although one barrel of his shotgun
was loaded and I'd witnessed how effectively he operated
as a one-man extermination squad, I saw him as a
saviour, not a threat. The Sandhurst accent suggested an
officer and a gentleman and so did his appearance. His
features were much more finely chiselled than those of his
dead fellow countrymen. He was also thinner than his
height would have suggested and his hair was greying at
the temples. More important, the bitterness in his face
had nothing to do with me.

'How about untying me?' I suggested. 'I can't say I'm
exactly comfortable here.'

'All in good time.' My discomfort evidently wasn't of
any immediate concern. 'First of all, tell me how you
came to be here.'

While I explained I marvelled at the apparent lack of

curiosity of the other occupants of the house. Not only were there no police sirens but no sounds of disturbance or excitement of any kind. Either the radio must have drowned the noise or shotguns were a feature of the normal daily grind in this area of Notting Hill.

Inevitably, my explanation led us on to more sensitive territory. He covered more or less the same ground as Mukwaya had done the previous day but Kironde was less inclined to accept evasions as an answer. For my part, I'd no intention of trying to be clever while I was strapped securely to a chair. I not only told Kironde that I was working for Sir Keith, I passed on the little I knew about what I'd been hired to do. Although Kironde pressed for more details about the body I was supposed to be guarding, I couldn't help him, and he had the sense to realize why. Presumably he'd found himself in situations where subordinates were told no more than it was absolutely necessary for them to know.

I knew I must have satisfied him when Kironde at last unstrapped me from the chair. While I rubbed away at my wrists and ankles, trying to get the circulation started again, he made sure I realized I wasn't an entirely free agent.

'Mukwaya's death doesn't alter anything,' he said. 'The sole difference is that you report to me instead of him.'

This wasn't something I was going to argue about.

'How do I contact you?'

'Don't worry, Philis.' Kironde's smile was devoid of humour. 'I'll be in touch with you. And please try to remember one thing. I don't ask for, or even want, your friendship, but I do expect total loyalty from the people I employ. Don't make the mistake of trying to feed me false information. I'm not a very tolerant man.'

I only had to look at the two dead bodies to appreciate what he meant. They were all I had to look at after Kironde had gone. As there was still no sign of the police,

I myself was in no great hurry to leave. I might not have
the slightest idea what Kironde had been looking for but
his search had been perfunctory to say the least and I
hoped I could do better. In the event, what I didn't find
was more significant than what I did. Neither man appeared to have carried any form of identification. There
were no passports, no driving licences, no envelopes with
names and addresses written on them.

They were as anonymous in death as they'd been alive.
I hoped the SR(2) disposal squad I'd called in would do
better when it arrived on the scene. Even if it didn't, it
would guarantee I had a lift back to headquarters. When
I reached there I was going to persuade Pawson to give
me some idea of what the hell was going on.

Charity wasn't a word which figured in Pawson's personal
vocabulary, and, according to departmental rumour, his
family motto was 'Never give unless you have already
received.' In fact, devising Pawson aphorisms seemed to
be a popular pastime at headquarters. Like 'He never,
ever kicks a man unless he's down' or 'The only reason
he'd help an old lady across the street is so he could mug
her on the other side'. It wasn't a game I'd ever played,
not out of any particular respect but because I didn't see
Pawson as a figure of fun. I saw him as the man who only
had to snap his fingers to pitchfork me into a situation
where my neck was on the line, and this wasn't the kind of
relationship which gave me many belly-laughs.

The important rule in dealing with Pawson was never
to be deceived by appearances. He was a chameleon with
a surface display to suit every occasion. Although he looked
like the personification of an English gentleman, his im-
maculately groomed exterior was nothing more than a
useful façade. Pawson had almost as many scruples as I
had udders. He combined total ruthlessness with an
analytical mind capable of the kind of tortuous devious-

ness which would have had Machiavelli applauding in admiration. He was also bloody good at his job and this was the main reason he remained the longest serving head of any British intelligence department. There were other reasons, of course. The missing Hoover files might be a modern American myth but I suspected that the Pawson Papers were a harsh reality. It would take a very brave Home Secretary to dismiss Pawson before he was good and ready to go.

Our discussion followed the usual pattern of such interviews. To begin with I did all the giving, running through the events of the past two days. While I talked, Pawson swung around in his swivel chair, fiddled with pencils and came out with the occasional enigmatic grunt, just to make sure I realized he knew far more than I did. It was knowledge he didn't impart easily. Instead of him giving me the explanation I was after, we had to play the guessing game. I had to be allowed every opportunity to draw conclusions which would show what a brainless idiot I was. Only then would Pawson share a few of the true facts with me.

'What do you make of it all, then, Philis?' Pawson enquired, initiating the process.

'Not a lot.' This was always a popular approach. Only Pawson and the Pope were infallible. 'As far as I can see, there are three separate groups involved, all working at cross-purposes. Apart from Sir Keith Tenby, there are two Ugandan organizations. One has connections with the present government in Kampala, the other is a hangover from Amin.'

Pawson had no intention of allowing me to escape so lightly. He didn't want a statement of the obvious. He wanted to tempt me into the area of idle speculation.

'The question is, what are they all after?'

'Your guess is as good as mine,' I said, determined not to be drawn. 'If Sir Keith is involved, there must be big money at stake. I'd say it's connected with whoever it is Thackeray and I are bringing into the country but that's as far as I can go. In any case, I didn't come here to play guessing games. I came here to listen to one of your masterly expositions.'

I should have known better. When it came to the unimportant background material, Pawson could be almost painfully thorough and he'd obviously been doing his homework on Amin. He took me right back to where he'd fought in Burma with the British in World War II and later in Kenya during the Mau Mau nastiness. He even threw in the bit about Amin being Ugandan heavyweight boxing champion. After Ugandan independence the ex-sergeant major's promotion had been rapid, and it wasn't long before Milton Obote had made him chief of staff. Six years later, in January 1971, Amin had repaid his benefactor by leading the coup which had deposed Obote.

To begin with Amin had been seen as a saviour, mainly because he'd given few hints of the monster he was destined to become. He'd even resorted to the standard ploy of all military dictators of promising the country free elections, going on record as saying Obote would be at perfect liberty to contest them. Obote, showing the common sense he'd lacked when he'd appointed his chief of staff, had wisely stayed where he was in Tanzania. Unlike his fellow countrymen, he'd had few illusions about what Amin was capable of.

Subsequent events had proved him more than right and Amin's honeymoon with the Ugandan people didn't last very long. However, it wasn't the assassinations and mass murders which interested Pawson. He was more concerned with the contribution Amin had made to the economic ruin of the country Churchill had once described as the pearl of Africa. The expulsion of the Ugandan Asians in 1972 and the takeover of all foreign-owned

companies the following year had effectively destroyed
the economic infrastructure of Uganda. Coffee and cot-
ton exports had been the basis of the country's wealth,
but without Asian and European marketing expertise, exports had soon dried to a trickle.

Within six years the ridiculous situation had developed
that with coffee prices at a record high and 2 million bags
of coffee stockpiled in Kampala for lack of purchasers,
the only coffee available within Uganda had had to be
imported. This was because all the coffee-processing fac-
tories within Uganda had ground to a halt for lack of
parts and skilled management. The same had been true
of sugar, another staple cash crop. From being a net ex-
porter of sugar, Uganda had become an importer because
the Asians who had run the sugar-mills had been de-
ported and there had been nobody to take their place.

However, there had been far more than simple economic mismanagement involved. Every prudent dictator
looked ahead to his old age, to the time when he might be
dictator no longer, and Amin had been no exception. At
the same time as Uganda had been sinking deeper into
the economic mire, Amin had been amassing his own personal fortune, and this was where Sir Keith Tenby had
come into the picture. Amin's sources of income might be
within Uganda itself but nobody in their right mind was
going to hoard Ugandan pounds unless they planned to
wallpaper their homes. Amin had wanted his money in
hard currencies, safely invested abroad, and he'd reached
an arrangement with Sir Keith. Amin had kept his hands
off Sir Keith's investments in Uganda and Sir Keith had
handled Amin's investments abroad. At least, this was the
way Pawson presented it to me.

'There has to be more,' I said.

'What do you mean?'

Pawson was wearing the smug expression I'd learned to
know and hate.

'I don't know what they are but Sir Keith's investments in Uganda can only be a drop in the ocean. At the most, they're only a sideline to what he's doing here. As far as Kironde's mob are concerned, there are an awful lot of people who did business with Amin, including our own revered government. The new regime in Kampala isn't going after them all. Like I said, there must be something more.'

Although Pawson wasn't actually clapping his hands, he seemed quite pleased with my efforts.

'You're definitely on the right lines, Philis,' he said approvingly. 'Perhaps I'd better tell you about the ruby mine.'

The whole business was beginning to sound like something straight from the pages of *Boy's Own*, but this didn't make me listen any the less attentively. I always listened very carefully when my life might be at stake.

The innocents of the whole affair had been two young American geologists, John Timmins and Elliot Parker. They'd been working out of Kapchorwa and they hadn't been looking for rubies. However, this was what they'd found in the band of crystalline limestone near Mount Elgon, and not just one or two of them either. When they'd completed their preliminary survey it seemed as though they might have hit upon the richest deposit of rubies outside Burma. Even their most conservative estimate suggested the deposit would be worth £10 million sterling and this had been three years ago, back in the days when the pound had been worth almost fifty pence.

The one major fly in the ointment was that so far Timmins and Parker were only rich on paper. Their fortune was still in the ground, ground ruled by Amin, and the American geologists hadn't completely ignored reality. They'd known they had problems and they'd had the

sense not to go around sounding off about their discovery
to everybody they met in the street. In fact, to begin with,
they hadn't told a soul. Operating the mine without official approval would have been impossible and neither
geologist had fancied applying for a permit. One of
Amin's favourite themes was keeping the wealth of Uganda
for Ugandans, or at any rate, for one Ugandan. In light of
this, it was most unlikely he'd allow a couple of young
Americans to leave the country with a fortune in rubies.

They'd needed working capital and they'd needed protection and it hadn't taken them long to decide where
they might find it. In a way they'd been semi-smart.
They'd gone for the only alliance which might have left
them rich and it wasn't really their fault that the gamble
hadn't paid off. Sir Keith Tenby was the sole foreign
national still making money in Uganda and it was common knowledge that he must enjoy some kind of special
relationship with Amin. Timmins and Parker had
calculated that if they brought him in on their deal, he'd
act as an effective buffer between them and the Ugandan
authorities. A slice of a fortune was infinitely preferable
to no fortune at all.

Timmins had been the one to stay in Kapchorwa while
Parker had flown to London to conduct the negotiations
with Sir Keith. At first the two Americans had had every
reason to feel pleased with themselves. Sir Keith's own
geologists had confirmed the potential of the deposit and
Sir Keith himself had been eager to participate. He'd held
out for 33⅓ per cent instead of the 25 per cent Parker
had originally offered but, against this, they were now as
fireproof as anybody could be in Uganda. The two
Americans still owned two-thirds of a ruby mine and Sir
Keith had promised to deal with the Ugandan authorities. It seemed they'd be able to sit back and watch the
money roll in.

Sad to say, they hadn't owned two thirds of a ruby mine

for very long. Pawson was at some pains to explain that
there was no question of any double-dealing on Sir Keith's
behalf. He'd adhered rigidly to the terms of the bargain
he'd struck with Parker and it hadn't been his fault he was
unable to deliver everything he'd hoped. Timmins and
Parker's two thirds share had been cut in half when Sir
Keith's representative in Kampala had completed the
delicate arrangements for a mining permit. Although
Amin had given his go-ahead, he'd been adamant that he
should receive his slice of the cake. His price for the permit had been 33⅓ per cent. It was to go to a group of
hand-picked local participants, although they were
nothing more than a front. All the profits would be going
direct to Amin himself.

Once again, this hadn't been a development the
American geologists had appreciated but they'd been
realistic enough to know they were still ahead of the
game. Sir Keith was putting up the capital, Amin was
supporting the project and a third share was more than
enough to make them rich.

They hadn't fully realized their own naïveté until six
months later, round about the time the first rubies were
being brought out of the limestone. Then, without any
warning, Timmins was declared a 'prohibited immigrant'
and allowed a paltry three hours to leave the country. He
left, protesting bitterly, and Parker had gone under-
ground, hoping against hope that Sir Keith would be able
to bail him out. It was a vain hope. Sir Keith was fully
occupied protecting his own investment, trading heavily
on the fact that Amin still relied on his expertise in the
world money markets. A week later Parker joined his
friend on the list of prohibited immigrants and, after a
month in hiding, he too left Uganda. He'd sensibly decided that his life was worth more than any number of
rubies.

It was an affair which had received wide coverage in

both the Ugandan and American newspapers. Amin, never the most reticent of men, had been more than willing to justify his stance. Referring to the ruby mine, he'd publicly reiterated his view that no foreigner should be allowed to exploit Ugandan resources for his own benefit. As a general principle it was fine but it skated over Sir Keith's continued participation in the venture. It had also ignored another self-evident fact, that the proceeds of the mine were destined for the private pockets of Amin and his select band of cronies.

Although American representatives did make vague noises about the high-handed treatment of Timmins and Parker, they made no progress. The Ugandan authorities simply countered with the accusation that the geologists had been gemstone smuggling and were lucky not to have ended up in jail. Furthermore, the Ugandan Ministry of Natural Resources had flatly denied that Timmins and Parker had had anything to do with the discovery of the rubies. As proof they produced photostats showing that the claim was registered in the name of one of Amin's appointees. Cynics might talk about pages being torn from the claims book but this didn't alter the reality. Timmins and Parker had been comprehensively shafted.

However, all this was simply the background, the lead-in to what really interested Pawson. Production at the mine had only just got under way when the first Tanzanian troops had crossed the Ugandan border. Suddenly, Amin had had far more important things to think about than rubies and so had the local government officials. Mount Elgon had been a long way from the fighting, so production had continued without interruption, but the mine had been operating in a virtual limbo. Nobody was quite sure for whom the rubies were being dug out of the ground so they had been stockpiled until the situation had clarified. This had continued throughout the long, confused months of fighting and it hadn't been until the

new regime was installed in Kampala that anybody had
had time to worry about the mine. By then it was too late
because there was no longer a stockpile of rubies to worry
about.

'I see,' I said, stubbing out my fifth cigarette of the session. 'You think Sir Keith removed the rubies for safe-
keeping.'

'That's what the Ugandans seem to think and they
should be in a position to know. It certainly makes sense.
Sir Keith had a legal claim to one third of the mine and
the owners of the other shares were far too busy saving
their own skins to argue about what was going on. As you
may have gathered, his stock with the new government is
none too high so his Ugandan holdings don't appear to
have a very bright future ahead of them. He may well
have decided to grab what he could while he could.'

'I see.' This was rapidly becoming one of my favourite
phrases. 'Is this mysterious person I'm supposed to be
looking after carrying the rubies? If so, he's taken a hell of
a long time getting from Uganda.'

'I know, Philis. That's one of the aspects which has
been puzzling me. All the same, it's the only assumption I
have to work on. At the moment nobody seems to have
any idea where the missing rubies are.'

'How much are they worth?'

'There again, I can't be sure. The figures I've heard
quoted range between three and five million.'

'Dollars?'

'No, pounds.'

I nodded nonchalantly. After all, on my salary who was
going to be impressed by a few million?

'Let's assume you're right,' I said. 'What am I supposed
to do? Retrieve the rubies?'

'On the contrary, Philis.' Pawson allowed himself a
smirk of self-satisfaction. It was a characteristic which invariably meant trouble for somebody. 'I shall expect you

to do exactly what Sir Keith has hired you to do. He can be very useful to me and a little bit of leverage never does any harm.'

Of course it didn't. In Pawson's book it was every bit as useful as a trip with Philis into Fantasy Land. There would be some missing rubies, because this was something I could easily check, and Pawson probably was after Sir Keith Tenby but this was about all I could be sure of. Pawson had only given me part of the story, just enough to keep me off his back, and I was prepared to bet that the real stakes would be considerably higher.

SAN REMO, ITALY

Perhaps all Africans were thick. Perhaps they were all stupid, tribal gangsters like the man in Genoa. Franco couldn't really say because he'd never talked to anybody else from the wrong side of the Mediterranean. Although Franco had disliked the man on sight, he'd taken great care to be polite. He always was when money was involved and business wasn't good enough for him to query its source. Besides, the Ugandan had looked perfectly capable of breaking an arm or a leg if Franco had upset him.

'I want you to find a woman for me,' he'd said once the introductions were completed.

'Any particular woman?'

Franco thought he'd been quite restrained, but his flippancy brought a frown to the African's face.

'Of course. I have a photograph of her here.'

After he'd examined the snapshot, Franco allowed himself a low whistle of appreciation. It was enough to earn him another frown.

'Is there a name to go with this?' Franco asked quickly,

trying to look like the conscientious businessman he pur-
ported to be.

'There is but it's immaterial for your purposes. She'll be
using an assumed name.'

The whole proposition had stunk to high heaven but,
with a landlord and mistress to support, Franco couldn't
afford to be fussy. There was a lot more guff to listen to
before he was able to leave. The Ugandan had stressed
how important it was to find the woman quickly. He'd
also stressed how clever and resourceful she was. Six of his
men had been searching for her for three weeks without
any success.

Franco had switched off for most of the briefing. The
only valuable piece of information was the general area
where she was thought to be hiding. There was nothing
else he needed. If he couldn't find her inside seventy-two
hours, he'd give up playing at private investigators and go
back to the drudgery of the *carabinieri*. Judging by the
photograph, he should be able to find the woman simply
by looking for the queue of slavering men outside her
door.

In actual fact, once he'd been allowed to go, it had
taken Franco half an hour on the telephone to establish
where she was and just over an hour on the motorway to
reach San Remo. Now he was sitting on the hotel terrace,
sipping his Campari while he watched her eating dinner
in the restaurant. The other six men who had been looking for her must have been able to add their IQs together
and still come up with a two-digit total.

Franco's only real problem was what to do now he'd
found her. He reminded himself that he had the mystique
of the private detective to consider. It would never do to
make the job appear too easy. There were expenses to be
considered as well. Reporting back so soon would leave
him very little scope for padding his bill.

It was far better left until the morning, Franco decided. At the very least, the delay should do something to ease his conscience. The girl at reception had been most helpful once he'd slipped her a few lire and she'd told him that 'Miss Baker' would be leaving in the morning. Provided she left early enough, she should have some kind of a start. Although Franco always tried to give value for money, he didn't believe in throwing in any extras. And when it came to a choice between Beauty and the Beast, Franco was on Beauty's side every time. He just hoped the woman was every bit as clever and resourceful as the Ugandan had maintained.

CHAPTER 5

Business was brisk at the Nice-Cote d'Azur Airport. Even so, I didn't have any difficulty spotting Thackeray. He stood head and shoulders above most of the tourists scurrying around him and he saw me at the same moment I located him. We exchanged waves, then I started pushing my way towards him. I didn't push too hard because there were a lot of short tempers in the airport that morning. The French flight controllers were in dispute again and the miasma of ruined holidays hung over the concourse. My own flight had had to be rerouted via Iceland and Cape Town or something equally ridiculous and I wasn't in a much better mood than the owners of most of the feet I trampled on.

Once I reached Thackeray he grabbed one of my suitcases and broke a path for me through the last ranks of holidaymakers standing between us and freedom. He didn't attempt to speak until we were out in the car park. The Porsche Carrera was the same shade of burgundy as the one he'd driven in England but the licence plates were French. Perhaps Sir Keith paid Thackeray enough for him to buy them by the half-dozen.

'I gather you didn't have too good a flight,' he said, swinging my suitcases into the boot.

'I was a bit pissed off when we flew over the Pole the second time.'

I never had been one to exaggerate. Thackeray came out with the happy, carefree laugh of somebody who had crossed the Channel by ferry and travelled the rest of the way by first-class sleeper. He'd not only be more rested than me, he'd have reached Nice in half the time it had taken me by air. If I'd spent much more time hanging around at Gatwick, I'd have established squatter's rights.

'Any bother?' he enquired, making a racing change as a couple of French pedestrians dived for safety at the car park exit.

'I took adequate precautions, if that's what you mean,' I told him. 'Nobody followed me.'

'Good.'

Thackeray probably wouldn't have been quite so satisfied if he'd known of my encounter with the SRB bully-boys. This was why I'd decided not to tell him. All he needed to know was that I was in contact with Kironde and had fed him the information Sir Keith had prepared for me.

Instead of driving into Nice, Thackeray turned the Porsche left through Cagnes-sur-Mer, then headed away from the coast on the Grasse road. I half expected to leave the main road at some point but Thackeray drove all the way into Grasse itself. Apart from a couple of casual remarks about the carefully tended plots of flowers we passed and about perfume in general, he wasn't communicative and I didn't attempt to start any conversations of my own. When Thackeray was at the wheel he liked to concentrate and I left him to it.

Our hotel was around the corner from the Musée Fragonard and it had enough staff for me to keep my hands in my pockets while the suitcases were brought from the car. I kept them there while the tips were being doled out as well. It was Thackeray's party and I failed to see why I should help to subsidize it. After I'd made sure I'd grabbed the more comfortable of the two beds, I lay back and waited until the porter had gone before I voiced my misgivings.

'I thought we were supposed to be undercover,' I said.

'That is the general idea.'

Thackeray had already started to unpack some very expensive toiletry from his pigskin suitcase.

'Well, we're not doing too well so far. If anybody really wants to find us, we've left a trail a mile wide for them to follow. Provided they know the ropes and have the right contacts, it won't take them more than twenty-four hours to catch us up.'

'In twenty-four hours we'll be gone. We're only staying here overnight.'

'So this isn't our base?'

'I do have a little more sense than that, Philis.' Thackeray's grin was entirely amiable. 'Let me get my clothes sorted and I'll explain over a drink.'

It seemed like a good idea. When he'd finished I'd know whether I'd been right not to tell Kironde I was going to the sunny South of France.

Thackeray's explanation didn't include anything about ruby mines and I hadn't expected it to. He was a general briefing the troops and the realm of high strategy was his and Sir Keith's preserve. All I had to manage was the do or die bit.

In fact, the way Thackeray explained what we had to do, everything was remarkably straightforward. The body we were supposed to be guarding would be crossing the Italian frontier at twelve o'clock the next day. Although no names were mentioned, it was going to be a female

body because none of the other reasons I could think of
for Thackeray referring to it as 'she' seemed applicable.
She would have her own vehicle, a yellow BMW 732, and
we would be waiting to provide an escort just east of Menton. We'd be using two cars ourselves, the Porsche and a
Datsun 280. As soon as we'd established contact,
Thackeray would slot in ahead of her while I brought up
the rear of the convoy. Our immediate destination would
be a hideaway near Gattières where we'd be spending the
following forty-eight hours. After that would come the
long drive across France to the Channel coast where a
boat would be awaiting us. Once we were safely in
England, my part would be over.

The whole business sounded almost like a holiday
jaunt. This was why I was so pleased when Thackeray
asked me if I had any questions. To begin with I tried the
easy ones, asking if we had a timetable to work to.

'No.' Thackeray was categoric. 'We take as long as
necessary. Our only priority is to make safe delivery in
England. The boat will stay where it is until I say otherwise.'

'Fine. Am I correct in assuming we're in a high-risk
area at the moment?'

'As far as we're concerned, the whole of France is a
high-risk area. We can't afford to be careless.'

'That isn't quite what I meant.' Thackeray knew this
already but I didn't object to spelling it out for him. 'Our
package wasn't hatched at the Italian frontier. She's been
travelling from somewhere or other and you obviously
think she may have company. I was wondering why we
don't assume responsibility until she's in France.'

A long, slow sip at his cognac was all the time
Thackeray needed to decide what he was going to tell me.
I knew he was going to lie before he opened his mouth.
Our charge had an escort with her in Italy and for the last
week they'd been holed up outside San Remo. The op-

position, which Thackeray still wasn't naming, had been getting uncomfortably close so the two had gone to ground until assistance had arrived. Now we'd arrived, my predecessor as bodyguard was going to arrange a diversion which should leave the road to the frontier clear. Once again, Thackeray wasn't giving details, but the impression he tried to give was that the diversion was only going to buy us an hour or two's grace. This was the reason for the switch he'd set up in Menton itself, and for going to ground again almost immediately.

The impression I received was an entirely different one. I didn't think Thackeray had any idea what had been happening in Italy and he'd only fabricated his little story to convince me he was in control. In any case, one aspect of what we were doing didn't make any kind of sense at all.

'What's wrong with an airlift?' I asked. 'Sir Keith could have chartered an entire fleet of aeroplanes for what he's paying me and it would have saved all this buggering around.'

The face Thackeray pulled wasn't a happy one.

'The lady doesn't like aeroplanes,' he said. 'As far as she's concerned, birds are the only creatures which are supposed to leave the ground.'

'So slip something into her afternoon tea,' I suggested. 'There's no need for her to wake up again until she's safely in England.'

'It may come to that, Philis, but it's strictly a last resort. She isn't a lady we can afford to offend.'

'OK.' I was pressing the conversation now, eager to move on before Thackeray realized how much he'd let slip. 'How about the opposition? I always like to know a little about the men I may have to kill.'

'They're scum, the dregs of the earth.'

'And that's an objective assessment?'

Thackeray had spoken with a bitterness he now

acknowleged with a wry smile. For a moment he'd sounded uncannily like the Ugandan, Kironde.

'There may have been a tiny bit of personal prejudice mixed in,' he admitted, 'but an international consensus wouldn't be all that different. The men we may have to cope with are some of the riff-raff who used to surround Amin. If it does come to killing, nobody is going to mourn for them. In any case, as I keep saying, I'm hoping there won't be any confrontation. If everything goes according to plan, there shouldn't be any trouble.'

If everything went according to plan, I'd be ruling the world and what had happened in London had hardly been an encouraging start. In my experience, once an operation turned sour, it stayed sour, and this was an operation which appeared to have curdled long before I'd become involved.

'There she is,' Thackeray said, hitting the handle of the passenger door. 'You know what to do.'

The identification hadn't really been necessary. There hadn't been any other mustard-yellow BMWs on the road all morning, and no vehicles of any description with an attractive Ugandan at the wheel. By the time she was level with where we'd parked, Thackeray was settling into the driving seat of the Porsche and he pulled away almost immediately, leaving a small cloud of dust lingering in the air behind him.

I waited another couple of minutes before I switched on the ignition of the Datsun and headed towards Menton. The sun was beating down and the Mediterranean looked blue and clean, which all went to show how deceptive appearances could be. I already knew that if there had been a diversion, it hadn't been successful. The good news was that there'd only been one man, another Ugandan, in the Peugeot which had been slotted in three cars behind the yellow BMW. Unfortunately, where one man was following, reinforcements weren't likely to be far behind. The possibility wasn't enough to make me hurry. Thackeray's instructions had been specific and so far I didn't have any reason to doubt their wisdom.

When I reached Menton I turned right off the main coast road, going through the tunnel and following a loop which brought me back down to the Quai Bonaparte. The driver of the Simca, who had been saving my parking space for me, moved off as soon as he spotted me in the rear-view mirror and I took his parking place. So far everything was proceeding according to plan. From where I sat, I had an unobstructed view of the café on the far side of the road. I could see the Ugandan woman sitting at one of the pavement tables, sipping her coffee as though she intended to make it last for the full fifteen minutes Thackeray had asked for. I could see her car, parked further along the kerb.

There was only one thing I couldn't see and this, for the moment, was probably the single most important element in the jigsaw. It seemed time for a spot of initiative so I lit myself a Gauloise, coughed up a few bits of lung and left the Datsun. It was no more than ten yards to the corner and as soon as I reached it, I realized I needn't have worried. The Peugeot had had to travel a few yards closer to Nice before it found a parking space but it was there and so was its driver. He was busy at one of the public telephones, contacting associates who were, I hoped, still in Italy.

I sauntered back up the hill to my car and settled down behind the wheel again. Five minutes later the woman paid her bill, then went inside the café to the toilet. This was where the switch was made and it was neatly done. The woman who came out of the cafe was the same size and colour as the woman who had gone in and wearing the same clothes. She was about to drive off in the same BMW. It should have been sufficient to convince anybody, but the man in the Peugeot was going to have a clear view of her face as she drove past him and this could ruin everything.

First indications suggested I was worrying unnecessarily. I allowed the BMW a few seconds start, then idled around the corner in time to see the Peugeot setting off in pursuit. The acid test came after we'd left Menton behind us. If the Ugandan's suspicions had been aroused, he should have moved in closer, possibly overtaken the BMW, but he seemed perfectly content to maintain his distance with a couple of other cars between him and his quarry. I kept the same distance behind him and the three of us drove in convoy through Monte Carlo and Nice. When we reached the Gattières turn-off, heading up into the mountains, my part was over. The BMW and its shadow continued along the coast road, towards Cagnes-sur-Mer, Cannes, Marseilles and all points west while I pulled into the side of the road. It seemed as though the bait had been swallowed. All that remained was to make sure Thackeray hadn't run into any difficulties.

He arrived twenty minutes later, swinging off to the right without even a glance in my direction. However uncomfortable she might have been, his travelling companion was maintaining a low profile in the back. I couldn't see a sign of her even though I knew she must be there. I waited another couple of minutes, just to satisfy myself that none of the following vehicles turned right as well, then set off after him. Perhaps I'd been wrong. Perhaps we really were going to have as smooth a ride as Thackeray had predicted.

I wasn't really certain whether or not I approved of Thackeray's choice of a hideaway. From one point of view it couldn't have been bettered. The chalet was totally isolated, built at the end of its own private drive with the nearest neighbours almost a mile away. Furthermore, the drive was the only way it could be approached without a long and arduous hike through the woods. In this sense it was the ideal place to go to ground for a day or two.

All the same, I still had my reservations. If I'd been looking for somebody in the area and trying to pinpoint potential hiding places, the chalet would have been one of the first possibilities I'd have circled on the map. And if we did have unexpected visitors, our very isolation was going to tell against us. Thackeray and I would have to cope entirely on our own because all manner of unpleasant deeds could be perpetrated at the chalet without any of the neighbours being disturbed. Perhaps I was quibbling but it had all been a little too easy for my peace of mind. Until we were safely back in London I'd be expecting a ruddy great bunch of bloodthirsty Ugandans to descend on me at any moment.

Once I was inside the kitchen I temporarily shelved my gloomy forebodings. It was immediately apparent that I'd been doing the original driver of the BMW a grave injustice when I'd decided she was attractive. While she'd been behind the wheel of the car, and later on in the café, she'd been too far away for me to fully appreciate how much good a dash of Indian blood did her. Now I was actually in the same room with her I could see that she was one of those racial cocktails which seemed to work so well. She was tall and she was black and she was beautiful and I might have fallen in lust with her at once if I hadn't caught the unguarded expression on her face as I came through the door. It only lasted a second or so but a second was plenty of time for me to catch the sheer malevolence. It wasn't the cool mountain air which had sent a shiver down my spine. If it should come to dropping some knockout pills in her bedtime Horlicks, this was a task I intended to leave to Thackeray. Either that or I was going to make damn sure I was a long way away when she woke up again.

'Meet Kuldip,' Thackeray said. Release from tension was making him expansive and jovial. 'Is everything OK?'

'It appears to be.' Shaking hands seemed inappropriate so I'd contented myself with a nod in Kuldip's direction. 'I suppose you saw the tail.'

'He'd have been hard to miss. He was on his own, wasn't he?'

'For the time being, but I don't know how long that will last. He telephoned for help while Kuldip was doing her party piece in Menton.'

Thackeray grimaced.

'Do you think he spotted the switch?'

'I wouldn't say so. When I last saw him he was still sticking to the BMW like a limpet.'

'That's a relief.' Thackeray had put any temporary apprehension aside. 'In any case, we'll know for sure tonight.'

'What was that you said?'

I was hoping I'd misunderstood Thackeray's meaning.

'Andrea is going to phone through from Marseilles tonight.' Thackeray seemed totally unaware of his error. 'We'll know how it went then.'

'And what if things have gone wrong? What if the switch has been spotted?'

Although I was addressing Thackeray, the most notice-able reaction was coming from Kuldip. Her hunted-animal expression was back in place and she was looking every bit as dangerous as she had done when I'd stepped through the door.

'Is she phoning through here?'

This was more of a demand than a question and she sounded as dangerous as she looked.

'Hold it, hold it.' Thackeray had his hands up in a placatory gesture. 'I'm not as big an idiot as you two appear to think. Andrea phones from Marseilles to a con-tact in Nice, then I phone the contact so he can hand on

the message. Nobody knows about this chalet apart from
Sir Keith and the three of us.'

I supposed this was an answer of sorts and I didn't dole
out any more portions of pessimism. It was easier to cross
my fingers and pray that Andrea was still a free agent
when she made her phone call. If she wasn't, we were likely
to discover that Nice was uncomfortably close for comfort.

MARSEILLES, FRANCE

Marc wasn't particularly surprised when the African
walked through the door of the hotel. He'd reached an
age where nothing much surprised him any more and big
Africans were two a penny around the docks, even if most
of them weren't as ugly as this one.

'I want a room,' the African said in English.

Marc pushed the hotel register across the counter and
accepted the man's documents in exchange. It seemed he
was Ugandan, and this was unusual.

'It's room 30,' Marc told him. 'Third floor opposite the
stairs. You pay in advance.'

It always was payment in advance, regardless of
whether or not the customer had any luggage. The Ugandan paid without comment but he wasn't yet ready to go
to his room.

'I'm looking for this woman,' he said, producing a
rather dog-eared photograph. 'She's driving a yellow
BMW.'

Marc only glanced at the photograph before handing it
back.

'You won't find any women round here with expensive
cars,' he said.

Nearly all the women Marc knew wore too much make-up and spent a lot of time swinging their handbags in doorways. It was these women who brought the hotel most of its trade.

'A friend told me you were the man to see. I know the woman is here in Marseilles because I followed her. Then she gave me the slip.'

Marc sucked his teeth while he considered the proposition. The Ugandan helped him to his decision by pushing a couple of banknotes across the counter.

'OK,' he said. 'Leave the photograph with me and I'll see what I can do.'

Marc didn't think Martel would be interested but he ought to pass the information on just to cover himself. It was as well he did. When three other Ugandans arrived in Marseilles later in the day, all of them looking for the same woman, Martel became very interested indeed.

The Ugandan Martel had picked up off the street was no problem at all. It only took an hour of gentle persuasion in the basement before he began to talk and once he started there was no stopping him. Most of what he had to say didn't concern Martel at all but as soon as he mentioned the rubies, the whole nature of the operation changed. Martel had already passed on the word to keep an eye open for a beautiful black woman in a yellow BMW, but this was no longer adequate. Now he had all his men out on the street, actively searching, and Martel even roped in a few of his contacts at police headquarters. It took less than an hour to locate the car but by then the woman was no longer with it. She wasn't found until after nightfall and she was taken straight to Martel.

It proved to be an unrewarding encounter. Not only was she the wrong woman but she hadn't even heard of the rubies. All she could give Martel was an account of what had happened in Menton and a telephone number in Nice. It was time for Martel to use a few more of the

contacts which extended all along the Riviera and as far
north as Paris. Now fortune had dealt him into the game,
Martel was there to stay.

CHAPTER 6

English gentlemen didn't stoop to pressing their ears
against doors or peeping through keyholes and nor did
I. There wasn't a great deal of point when the built-in
wardrobe was so convenient. Although Thackerary had
accompanied Kuldip into her bedroom, I wasn't in the
wardrobe to monitor their sex life or pick up any tips on
technique. Their relationship was cordial but cool, with a
definite reserve on both sides. Besides, if they had had
anything going, Thackeray would hardly have been shar-
ing a bedroom with me.

This was where the wardrobe was, in my bedroom, and
there was only a hardboard partition separating it from a
similar wardrobe in Kuldip's room. Although they were
talking in low voices and reception wasn't everything I'd
have liked, even using the detachable shower unit I'd
brought from the bathroom, it didn't take me long to pinpoint the main reason for their mutual reserve. I'd missed
the first few exchanges in their discussion and I still wasn't
pinning too much faith on Pawson's briefing, but it was
an interesting conversation none the less.

'So you don't have them with you?' Thackeray was saying.

'No way.' Kuldip said this with a laugh. 'I'm vulnerable
enough as it is.'

'They are safe, though?'

Thackeray was evidently concerned.

'Don't worry. They're my future as well as yours. Once
I'm safely in England and your Sir Keith Tenby has met

his end of the bargain your troubles will be over.'

'You're safe enough now.' Thackeray might be fighting a losing battle but he was game. 'We're not going to allow anything to happen to you.'

'I know you're not.' Even through the partition, Kuldip's amusement came across clearly. 'You can't afford to.'

For the next few seconds neither of them spoke. Thackeray's first approach had been a total failure and I guessed he was casting around for an alternative. I seized the opportunity to remove a stray coat hanger from my ear and ease myself into a more comfortable position.

'Look, Kuldip,' Thackeray started again. 'I appreciate your situation but you really ought to try to understand ours. Where would we be left if there was an accident and something did happen to you?'

'At least I'd have the satisfaction of knowing somebody would be shedding a few tears for me.'

There was no doubt about it, she was a hard woman.

'You're missing the point. Sir Keith has made a considerable investment in your safety. He deserves some guarantee of a return on it. At the moment he's left holding the short end of the stick.'

'My heart bleeds for him.' Kuldip was unmoved. 'Besides, he does have a guaranteed return on his investment provided I reach London safely.'

'But you're not going to be cast to the wolves even if you do share your secret with me now.' Thackeray's irritation and frustration were beginning to show through. 'Sir Keith and I are men of our word. We promised to look after you and that's precisely what we'll do, regardless of any other considerations. You do trust us, don't you?'

'Of course I do. I have absolute faith in your self-interest.'

Their conversation continued along the same lines for another minute or two, travelling round and round in ever-diminishing circles. I preferred not to wait to see whether or not it reached its probable destination. I'd been detailed to brew the coffee while they were having their little heart-to-heart and this was a task I now completed. I didn't feel I was missing too much by leaving the built-in wardrobe. I'd learned as much as I was likely to and now I had a better picture of the overall situation, I could start making my own plans accordingly.

It began to seem as though my pessimism had been without foundation. Thackeray went out that night to make his phone call and returned well satisfied with what he'd heard. His contact in Nice had received the message from Marseilles on schedule. The opposition had bought the switch completely and the understudy's role was finished. She'd already ditched the man in the Peugeot and all she had left to do was lose herself, making sure she didn't leave a trail which could be followed.

Nor was there any unwarranted activity in the vicinity of the chalet. For almost forty-eight hours the three of us were in limbo. Apart from hearing the occasional car driving past on the road below, Thackeray and Kuldip passed their time in total isolation. They read, they ate, they slept and they had at least two disagreements on a familiar theme when they thought I was out of earshot.

For my part, I didn't spend nearly as much time inside the chalet. However, it wasn't loneliness, or even claustrophobia, which drove me into the great outdoors. I knew all about safe houses. I knew what it was which earned them their nomenclature and, in one important respect, the chalet fell way short of requirements. Admittedly, the main element which made a house safe was that nobody with hostile intentions knew anything about it and on this score I couldn't fault Thackeray's choice. It also looked as though his prediction had been correct, that the opposition had gone steaming off to Marseilles leaving us in the clear. So far there had been absolutely nothing to suggest otherwise.

On the other hand, I knew something of the basic psychology which was associated with safe houses like the chalet. They made people feel relaxed and secure. They made them complacent. The people inside them tended to lower their guard and they became vulnerable if the unexpected should occur. This was why it was so vital for every safe house to have a second element to it and in this respect our hideaway was sadly deficient. There was no bolt hole. If the worst should happen, there was no back way out, no line of retreat ready prepared.

Although I realized that I was probably wasting my time, I'd been trained to be thorough. More important, it was something which would have been niggling away at the back of my mind all the time we were at the chalet. This was why I was up bright and early the morning after our arrival, hiking up the mountainside through the trees. The only map of the area that Thackeray had was worse than useless for my purposes but at least it did give me some idea of where I ought to be heading. By midday I'd climbed a couple of small mountains, I had blisters on both feet and I'd probably sweated off a couple of pounds in weight. On the credit side, though, I'd arrived where I wanted to be and I could actually pinpoint my position on the map. All that remained to round off the morning was to grow a few more blisters when I retraced my footsteps.

Over lunch I explained what I'd been doing. Neither Thackeray nor Kuldip actually applauded my efforts but they both seemed to appreciate my concern for their safety. I didn't bother to explain that it was my own peace of mind which had provided the motivation. After we'd finished eating, I spread the map out on the living-room floor and showed them where my escape route would take us. As Thackeray was quick to spot, it would leave us slap-bang in the middle of nowhere.

'We'd still have one hell of a walk ahead of us,' he pointed out.

'That all depends how stupid we are.'

My morning's exercise hadn't left me in the best of tempers and I was a trifle short with him. Kuldip didn't appear to notice.

'I can see what Philis means,' she said. 'If we took one of the cars round by road, we could leave it hidden in the woods.'

'Precisely,' I agreed. 'It may be an unnecessary precaution but it would give us some kind of an edge if anything should go wrong.'

Thackeray evidently thought it was an unnecessary precaution. On the other hand, he'd hired me because of my professional know-how and he wasn't the poor fool who would have to hike back over the mountain once the Datsun had been concealed. The only problem I had was in dissuading Kuldip from coming with me. Ever since the previous evening, when I'd intercepted a couple of speculative glances in my direction, I'd known that she had designs on my body. She'd also taken to standing or sitting closer to me than was strictly necessary, a development I hadn't allowed to go to my head, or any other part of me. The lady was feeling horny and as her dispute with Thackeray put him out of the running she wasn't left with a great deal of choice.

Fortunately, Thackeray was only too happy to solve the problem for me. When Kuldip made her suggestion, he quashed it immediately. Although, as her petulant pout showed, she didn't receive his judgment with particularly good grace, she could hardly argue with his reasoning. I wasn't going to attract a great deal of attention but she undoubtedly would. Cosmopolitan though the South of France might be, six feet tall Ugandan women weren't exactly thick on the ground.

Once this was sorted out, I was free to take the Datsun

from the garage, fill up the tank in Gattières and take a leisurely drive through the French countryside. Three miles on foot became more than ten miles by road but I saved time when I arrived because I'd already decided where to leave the car. Although I didn't park it in plain view, I didn't go to a great deal of trouble to hide it. The track leading up through the forest obviously hadn't been used for several weeks. In any case, in a little over twenty-four hours the Datsun should be an irrelevance and the screen of branches I erected to conceal it from the track should last for at least a day. After that I couldn't care less what happened to the car.

When I'd finished with the car, I set off on my third trek of the day. I'd hoped it would be my last but it was too late in the afternoon to do everything I wanted before it began to get dark. It was one thing to know where I intended to run in an emergency, quite another to know the best way of getting there. After I'd woken up the following day, entertained for the third morning running by Thackeray's impressive range of callisthenics, I nearly decided not to bother. All being well, we'd be leaving the chalet that night and it hardly seemed worth the effort, an attitude my poor abused feet heartily endorsed.

Over breakfast I decided that growing old was no excuse for growing sloppy. Besides, the prospect of a long morning cooped up with Thackeray and Kuldip didn't exactly thrill me to the marrow. As it turned out, the only reward for another four hours of hard walking was a few minutes shaved off the time it would take me to reach the Datsun. I hoped I wouldn't have occasion to find myself in a situation where this extravagant expenditure of energy became worthwhile.

Back at the homestead, Thackeray had been making preparations for the night ahead. I could tell from the maps spread all over the living-room floor. However, the briefing had to wait until we'd forced down another of the

scratch meals at which Kuldip excelled. Although she
hadn't argued when Thackeray had appointed her cook,
she hadn't accepted the post with any noticeable enthusiasm. Nothing she'd put on the table since then had
suggested any aptitude for domesticity. Her culinary
technique consisted of opening a few tins, slopping the
contents into a saucepan and heating them until they
turned brown. The results were edible without being at
all appetizing and if I'd had to face her cooking for long,
I'd soon have been sneaking out to the Auberge de Gattières down the road. She was the only woman I'd met
who actually cooked worse than I did myself.

After we'd all mucked in at the sink, Thackeray
gathered us around him in the living-room. However,
Kuldip was only present as a courtesy, because it was my
opinion he wanted. How we travelled was already decided. There was a Volkswagen camper in the garage
and, while it didn't have the speed of the Porsche, it was a
far better vehicle for our purposes. A plywood partition
had been fitted between the seats at the front and the
main body of the vehicle, and all the windows at the back
had been covered with reflecting tint to guarantee our
privacy. Better still, the camper would make us completely independent of hotels.

What Thackeray hadn't told me was where we were heading and which route we'd be following. The maps suggested
that he still hadn't committed himself. He'd been leaving his
options open until the last possible moment.

'This is where we're going,' he said.

His finger was indicating a point on the French Channel coast between Le Havre and Fécamp.

'Is that where the boat is waiting?'

'It is.'

Kuldip pulled a face.

'I don't like boats,' she announced. 'They make me
sick.'

'But you do prefer them to aeroplanes.' Thackeray was patently lacking in sympathy. Two days of close proximity had done nothing to make their relationship blossom. 'You have to use one or other of them to cross the Channel unless you intend to swim.'

Just in case her contemptuous snort hadn't been expressive enough, Kuldip ostentatiously removed herself to the table where she started to lacquer her fingernails. For a moment I thought Thackeray was about to say something further, but he managed to hold himself in check. I was the one he wanted to talk to and he was perfectly under control when he turned back to the map. As he pointed out, the fastest route was to go through Fréjus and Aix-en-Provence to Avignon, then follow the motorway all the way to Pouilly. From there we could take the Autoroute du Sud to Paris and follow the Seine most of the way to the coast. However, this wasn't the route Thackeray was recommending. He was simply saying it was the most direct one and awaiting my comment.

'How long will the boat wait for us?' I asked.

Thackeray had told me once in Grasse but I wanted to make sure I'd heard him right.

'As long as necessary,' he answered. 'Scargill's instructions are to stay where he is until I instruct him otherwise.'

I nodded.

'Fair enough. If we're not operating to a timetable, I'd suggest we give the Rhône valley a miss. It's a little bit too obvious. The opposition may have lost the trail in Marseilles but they know roughly where Kuldip is heading. The motorway would be too easy for them to cover and the same goes for the N6. I think we ought to be a little more devious.'

Now it was Thackeray's turn to nod.

'The same thought had occurred to me, Philis. How about going to Grenoble, then cutting across to Paris from there?'

'Why not go the whole hog? As time is no object, why not miss Paris completely? Even if somebody does guess we're making for the Channel coast, they won't be expecting us to approach it from the north.'

We spent almost half an hour with our heads together, working out an itinerary. We eventually decided to drive round Paris to the east, travelling in a great loop which would take us to Amiens. After this it would only be a few miles to Dieppe where we'd turn south along the coast.

Once we'd settled this, it was simply a matter of waiting until nightfall so we'd have the cover of darkness for the first part of our journey. By morning we should be well out of any area the opposition might reasonably expect us to be in. At least, I thought it was simply a matter of waiting, until Thackeray announced he was going into Gattières to buy a few bits and pieces for the journey.

'Is that really necessary?' I asked. 'We already have most of the essentials aboard the Volkswagen. If we have forgotten anything, we can always pick it up along the way.'

'I want to make a phone call as well.' Although there was a telephone at the chalet, Thackeray had sensibly placed it off limits. 'I'm going to make a last check with my man in Nice. He's been keeping an ear to the ground to make sure we're still in the clear.'

Although I still thought Thackeray was taking an unnecessary risk, he was the boss and I had more important things to do than argue. Like catching up on some sleep for the long night ahead of us.

NICE, FRANCE

'What shall we do with him now?' Ferrier asked.

Martel didn't answer him immediately. He regretted having had to involve Ferrier, although he knew he'd had no real alternative. The man might be an animal but he made a dangerous enemy and Martel had never seriously considered moving into his territory without permission. The very last thing he wanted was any more headlines about gang warfare on the Riviera. His little house-cleaning back home in Maresilles had been prominently featured in newspapers all over the world and this was the kind of exposure he didn't need. Publicity put pressure on the police and they, in turn, put pressure on him, despite all the money he channelled into the department.

'What do you suggest, Henri?' he said, deciding to be diplomatic.

'Well, he's no further use to us. He's told us everything he knows.'

'True.'

It had been a messy business, but the man had talked in the end.

'We can hardly let him go,' Ferrier continued. 'I hear they're building a new road up near Grasse. We could give a little help with the foundations.'

'Do what you think best.' The disposal of bodies didn't interest Martel. 'What are you doing about the information he gave to us?'

'It's already in hand.' Ferrier sounded complacent. 'If he's right and the woman is still hiding in the area, I'll guarantee to find her inside twenty-four hours.'

'I may hold you to that.' Martel used threats sparingly but he thought it useful to remind Ferrier who was in charge. 'I can't do anything more here so I'll return to the villa.'

'Fine. I'll be in touch with you as soon as there's any news. Do you want any company to keep you amused while you're waiting?'

Although the conspiratorial leer on Ferrier's face irritated him, Martel's hesitation was only momentary.

'That's very hospitable of you, Henri,' he said. 'You know my tastes.'

Sure, Ferrier thought to himself. That's why I keep my daughter well out of your reach.

CHAPTER 7

I never did get any sleep. It wasn't for want of trying, though. I lay down on the bed and closed my eyes. I even started off the dream sequence about a cricket match at Lord's which should have bored me to sleep in a matter of seconds, but I hadn't made allowances for Kuldip. It was only five minutes after Thackeray had driven off in the Porsche that she was in the bedroom with me. Although, to be truthful, a large part of me was all in favour of what she had in mind, the rest of me was annoyed. It wasn't only women who didn't like to be taken for granted.

'Well?' she said, sitting on the edge of the bed.

'Well what?' I said helpfully.

The idiot approach wasn't going to last me for very long. We both knew I was fully aware of what Kuldip wanted and I strongly suspected she'd been right to take me for granted. I hoped she wasn't but I'd always had more than my fair share of human frailty. This was what was annoying me.

'You know, Philis,' Kuldip went on, the speculative glint still in her eyes, 'I receive the distinct impression that you've been trying to avoid me.'

'How very astute of you.'

'Why? Do I frighten you?'

The idea seemed to amuse her.

'No. At least, not in the sense you mean.'

'Has Thackeray warned you off, then?'

I shook my head.

'He hasn't said a word about not touching the goods.'

'So what's the problem? You're not racist, you're not queer and you're big enough yourself not to worry about my size. I've been making it as clear as I can that I'm available and you just keep on looking the other way. I don't think I'm flattering myself when I say most men would jump at the opportunity.'

'I'm sure they would, but I'm not most men. I'm your bodyguard. I suppose you could say it's a question of professional etiquette.'

'You mean I'm sacrosanct?' Kuldip was sounding amused again.

'That's putting it a bit strong. The thing is, I have to be objective about you if I'm going to do what I'm being paid for properly. Assuming the worst does happen and we do run into trouble, I don't want to find myself thinking about what a great lay you were the previous night. Personal involvement means inefficiency. Decisions start getting clouded. In certain situations it could literally make the difference between life and death. If you're still interested, look me up when we're safely in England and maybe we can put it together. Until then it's better for both of us if you stop bugging me.'

There were several ways I could have played it but this had seemed to be my best bet. If I could successfully disassociate Philis the man from Philis the bodyguard, I shouldn't ruffle too many feathers.

'I see,' Kuldip said.

When she stood up from the bed I thought she'd bought it. When she started to unbutton her blouse I realized I'd underestimated both her determination and her sexuality. It was going to take more than a few trite phrases to turn her off and this was all I had in stock. I'd made the gesture, I'd raised my token objections and now it was time to raise something else. OK, I knew she was dangerous and unpredictable. I realized I was probably only a substitute for a vibrator but none of this really mattered. Danger and unpredictability were what helped to make life worth living, and my libido wasn't talking in terms of a long-term relationship. It was demanding elemental sex, an urgent coupling with the sleek, black body which was being revealed to me as Kuldip slowly stripped.

'I'd rather you were subjective, Philis,' she was saying, filling in time while she undid buttons and zips and hooks. 'I want you to remember how good I am in bed. I'm going to make such an impression on you that you won't dare allow anything to happen to me. You're going to find out I'm just as addictive as heroin.'

At least, this was the gist of what she was saying, because I wasn't paying a great deal of attention. It was the actions which counted, not the words, and Kuldip couldn't have wished for a more appreciative audience. She stripped even better than I thought she would, revealing hectare after hectare of silky black skin. Once her pants hit the floor there was nothing else to uncover and Kuldip struck a pose which was mildly obscene and decidedly erotic. The next move was up to me and I rolled off the bed towards her, acutely aware of the animal odour of her as I moved closer.

'You'd better get dressed again, love,' I said, allowing myself one appreciative pat of a buttock. 'We don't want you catching cold.'

'You're turning me down?'

Kuldip sounded as though she couldn't believe it was happening to her.

'Something like that,' I agreed, taking my erection in the direction of the door.

'You bastard,' she began behind me. 'Of all the . . .'

I didn't hear the rest because the snarl of Thackeray's Porsche had communicated a sense of urgency to me the instant I'd picked it up in the distance. He was pushing

the car to the limit, driving up the hill like a bat out of
hell, and this could only spell trouble. By the time I
reached the living-room window he'd already turned into
the drive and I knew I hadn't been mistaken. Thackeray
exited from the Porsche at a dead run, not even stopping
to slam the door behind him, and I headed for the
kitchen to intercept him, only stopping long enough to
pick up a shotgun from the closet in the hall. I hadn't
noticed any signs of pursuit but some form of precaution
seemed appropriate.

'Where's Kuldip?' Thackeray demanded as he burst in
through the door.

'Getting changed, I think.'

He wasn't allowing me an opportunity to phrase any of
my own questions.

'Tell her to get her things together.' By now Thackeray
was brushing past me, on his way into the living-room.
'We may be leaving in a hurry.'

There was no need to pass on the message. Kuldip had
belatedly realized I'd had a good reason for resisting her
charms. She'd joined me in the doorway of the living
room, doing up the last buttons of her blouse as she looked
over my shoulder.

'What's happened?' she asked.

'I only wish I knew.'

Thackeray wasn't answering because he was too busy at
the telephone. When he'd finished dialling he held the
receiver to his ear for almost a minute before he replaced
it and turned to face us.

'Armand isn't there,' he said.

'How serious is that?'

Although I knew Armand was Thackeray's contact in
Nice, this was about all I did know. I didn't have enough
information to form an independent evaluation of the
situation.

'He's very reliable.' Despite his obvious concern,

Thackeray was picking his words with care. 'His instructions were to make sure he was available to answer the telephone at all times. In any case, he knew I was going to be in touch with him this afternoon. He would have made sure he was there.'

'So you think something has happened to him?'

This was called stating the obvious and I was glad Kuldip had got in ahead of me.

'I'm sure of it. The question is, do we stick to schedule or do we leave now?'

The question was for me alone and I still didn't know nearly enough to come up with a sensible answer. All I could do was put the ball back into Thackeray's court.

'A quarter of an hour isn't likely to make a great deal of difference either way,' I said. 'Why don't we think about it while I take a look round outside?'

Fifteen minutes could make a hell of a difference, but so could driving straight into an ambush. The sweep I did around the chalet was rudimentary to say the least and I didn't flush any suspicious characters from behind the trees. More important, I didn't find anything to suggest there had been any suspicious characters there before I'd started crashing through the undergrowth. Although this wasn't conclusive enough to guarantee my own peace of mind, the news went down well with Thackeray. By now he'd had a chance to recover his cool. To my mind he was a little too cool.

'It looks as though we're in the clear, whatever happened to Armand,' he said. 'He doesn't know the location of the chalet.'

'He does know we're still somewhere in the area,' I pointed out.

'That leaves an awful lot of square miles to cover.' I wasn't making any dents in Thackeray's new-found confidence. 'Perhaps I was over-reacting. I think we're better off proceeding as planned. That seems less of a risk than driving around the countryside in broad daylight.'

'Doesn't that rather depend on how long Armand has been missing? For all we know the opposition may have had almost forty-eight hours to narrow down the search area.'

I felt it was up to me to play devil's advocate. Whatever Thackeray might think, I wasn't at all happy with the situation. Things were beginning to turn sour again.

'The odds are still in our favour.' Thackeray had reached a decision and wasn't about to change his mind. 'If there are people out looking for us, they'll be covering as many roads as possible. There's no way they'll be able to spot us after dark.'

'Maybe,' I conceded, 'but why don't we cover all the bets? We could go up over the mountain, stay in the Datsun until after nightfall and then make a break for it. That way we'd really be minimizing the risks.'

Unfortunately, Kuldip wasn't any keener on mountaineering than Thackeray himself. Although it didn't actually come to a vote, she made it plain that, whatever her designs on my body, it was Thackeray's judgment she trusted. In its own small way, this was an illustration of why democracy doesn't really work. Majority decisions don't necessarily equal correct decisions. However justified Thackeray's optimism might be, us practising pessimists were generally the ones to live to a ripe old age.

I spent most of the afternoon and early evening out in the woods looking for Ugandans and my failure to spot any didn't do a thing to swing me around to Thackeray's point of view. I hoped he was right and, on the surface, his thinking was logical enough. There was nothing to link the chalet with either Sir Keith or us, the search force would only be about half-a-dozen strong and, even if we assumed the worst, the opposition would only have had two days to pin us down.

This was the reasoning which had impressed Kuldip. On balance I had to agree that the odds were slightly in our favour, especially as the people looking for us would be operating a long way from home. On the other hand, I knew far more about finding people than either of my companions. Providing the right approach was used, it wasn't nearly as difficult as Thackeray seemed to think. In the same way, I didn't find the absence of overt observation any more reassuring. If we had been located and the opposition knew its job, they'd be waiting for darkness, just like us.

Thackeray must have had the odd doubt or two himself, because he made a couple more attempts to contact Armand. As neither of them was successful, the results were no more conclusive than those of my own expeditions into the woods. Kuldip seemed to be the least affected by the tension. She seemed perfectly content to spend the time touching up the lacquer on her toe- and fingernails. Either she had total faith in Thackeray and myself or she had better nerves.

By the time it was dark, I'd decided Thackeray had probably been right. He'd been sloppy and careless but he seemed to have got away with it and this was what counted. Even so, we didn't go out of our way to publicize our departure. As Thackeray knew the area much better than I did, he'd drawn first stint at the wheel. Kuldip and I clambered into the back before he drove out of the garage.

'All set?' he enquired, talking through the partition which separated him from us.

'We're fine,' I told him. 'Drive carefully.'

We weren't fine and Thackeray wasn't allowed an opportunity to drive carefully or otherwise. The joker with the submachine gun was hidden in the trees to the left of the drive, about halfway between the chalet and the road, and he didn't waste ammunition on a shot across our bows. There was enough reflected illumination from the headlights for him to see that Kuldip wasn't in the front and this was all the excuse he needed to empty his magazine at Thackeray.

One part of my brain was still registering the fact that he was probably using a M1949 as I dragged Kuldip to the floor, shielding her with my body while I listened to the 9mm Parabellums hammering into the driving section of the Volkswagen. My guess was that Thackeray must have died instantaneously. All I could hear was the smashing of glass and the staccato chatter of the submachine gun but Thackeray certainly wasn't steering any longer. Instead of negotiating the bend which would have taken us down to the road, the camper carried straight on, beating aside a couple of saplings before the front hit a trunk which wouldn't bend.

Kuldip was trying to say something as I pushed myself up but I ignored her. This wasn't a time for gallantry. It was a time for survival and I wasn't particularly gentle as I hauled her to her feet. Fortunately we hadn't been travelling fast enough for the camper to topple on its side when it had hit so there weren't any problems about getting out. All our problems would be waiting for us once we were in the open.

'I'm going out,' I said. 'You don't follow until I tell you to. Then you run like you've never run before. We're heading back to the chalet.'

I was working to a mental timetable which didn't allow for discussion or argument and I was already opening the door. The character with the M1949 had used a whole magazine on Thackeray and I hoped he was still reloading as I went out into the trees to join him. The first two rounds from the police model Remington removed a lot of bark and encouraged him to keep his head down while I angled out into the middle of the drive, risking the exposure in return for a clear shot at where he had to be.

I heard the sound I'd been dreading while I was a good three strides from where I needed to be, the unmistakable click as the cocking handle of the M1949 was pushed into its forward position. This was all the encouragement I needed to launch myself into a rolling dive which was going to give me a nasty attack of gravel rash and left me on my back on the ground, head pointing in the direction I wanted it to. He fired high, just as I knew he would. He wasn't so high, though, that I wanted him to improve with practice, and I fired twice at the muzzle flash. There was no way I could miss, not with the spread of the shotgun. He screamed once and horribly, then started threshing around in the undergrowth.

'Come on, Kuldip,' I bellowed. 'Run.'

As I bellowed I was rolling again because I didn't know how many others there were out in the dark but I wasn't at all shy about leaping to my feet as Kuldip steamed past. Although grabbing hold of her arm might have slowed us down a little, it made me feel a hell of a sight safer. Kuldip wouldn't be any use to anybody if she was dead, which meant I ought to be safe too so long as I stuck to her like a limpet. At least, this was the theory, and no more shots were fired at us on our dash back to the chalet.

Fortunately, Kuldip didn't know me well enough to understand the complex machinations of the Philis brain. She thought I'd been playing the Good Samaritan, extending the proverbial helping hand.

'Thanks,' she said.

She was leaning back against the wall and panting. I was doing my panting while I peered through the window to see what, if anything, was happening outside.

'Forget it,' I told her, 'and you'd better start saving your breath. You'll have some more running to do soon.'

'We're going to try for the Datsun?'

'Unless you can think of anything better. I don't see we have any choice.'

Nothing was happening outside. Or, if it was, it was happening somewhere I couldn't see it. This was no more than I'd expected, otherwise I'd never have stopped for a breather in the chalet. If the opposition had been ready for us, Thackeray would have been shot the moment he'd opened the garage door. This would have been a far easier method of making sure we didn't leave, with the added advantage that there would have been no risk of damaging Kuldip. We'd caught everybody on the hop and I hoped I'd calmed people down by returning to the chalet.

In any case, it didn't make a great deal of difference whether or not my assessment was correct. If by some chance the man with the M1949 had been entirely on his own, we were in the clear anyway. If, as seemed far more likely, he had friends with him, I should have blunted their sense of urgency. So long as we were safely cooped up, there was no need of precipitate action. They could make their dispositions secure in the knowledge of where we were.

'Make a phone call,' I said to Kuldip.

'What?'

Her tone of voice suggested she doubted the sanity of her sole remaining bodyguard.

'Lift up the receiver and listen,' I explained. 'I want to know whether the wires have been cut.'

It was only a few seconds before she was back beside me at the window.

'It's dead,' she told me.

'Fine,' I said. 'Here's what we're going to do.'

It was too, more or less. The only thing I didn't explain to Kuldip was that I'd be using her as bait.

NICE, FRANCE

'How old are you, my dear?'

'Thirteen, sir.'

Yvette was eighteen but she had the body and face of an adolescent and this was what the randy old goat was paying for. Ferrier had told her how important he was and she was prepared to play along with any cruddy scenario he chose.

'And you say you don't have anywhere to stay?'

'No, sir. My parents have thrown me out. They say they can't afford to support me any more.'

In real life, Yvette had left home when she was fifteen, just as soon as her stepfather had started jumping her every time her mother's back had been turned. It hadn't been that she'd objected to what he did to her. Being a practical girl, she'd simply wanted to capitalize on her assets.

'Don't you have any relatives who can help you?'

'They all live in the north, in Paris. That's why I've come to you.'

'Is that the only reason?'

It took another twenty minutes of infantile chatter before Yvette was stripping off and Martel was running her bath. Once she was in the water, having gone through all the coy, maidenly protests he'd expected, things speeded up a little. Martel lost much of his interest in the dialogue after he'd started soaping her, preferring to concentrate on the job in hand. Yvette had just decided they might actually make it into bed before the New Year when the telephone rang next door. Even then Martel didn't completely abandon his assumed role.

'I'm sorry, my dear,' he said, allowing his fingers one

last sweep through her carefully groomed pubic hair. 'I shan't be a moment.'

As she lay back in the water, Yvette hoped he was more direct on the telephone than he had been with her. Otherwise she'd end up looking like a prune. Although she could probably have heard what was being said if she'd tried, she was careful not to. She was a prudent girl and, in the circles she moved in, other people's secrets could be dangerous. She guessed this might be one such occasion when Martel returned to the bathroom. There was a new sense of purpose about him which made him a different proposition from the doddering old fool she'd been humouring a minute or two before.

'Get dressed,' he instructed her. 'I have to go out.'

Yvette was about to ask whether he wanted her to wait for him until she recognized the expression on Martel's face. Then she knew she'd be wasting her time. As her night's work had been paid for in advance, this didn't upset her in the slightest.

'What the hell does Ferrier think he's playing at?' Martel growled.

'Perhaps he didn't want to disturb you while you were enjoying yourself.'

The driver of the Citroën didn't take his eyes from the road when he spoke.

'There's more to it than that. I told him I wanted to know the minute the woman was found. How long did you say it was since he learned about the chalet?'

'It must be at least a couple of hours. I only heard about it by chance.'

'So what the hell does he think he's playing at?'

This time the driver didn't answer. He wasn't paid to make judgments. In any case, the question had been rhetorical. Martel knew exactly what Ferrier was doing. Despite Martel's specific instructions to the contrary, the

stupid prick was trying to show how efficient he was by
handling everything himself. If he was correct, and if Ferrier should make a mess of it, Martel promised himself
that the idiot was finished. There were plenty of people
all along the coast who would be only too happy to see
him go.

CHAPTER 8

There was bound to be somebody watching the back.
There had to be unless we were dealing with a bunch of
total incompetents. He, she or they would be stationed
back in the trees, posted there to make sure Kuldip and I
didn't sneak off before they were ready to come in and
take us. They'd be watching the windows and the doors
and they'd have been told that I was totally expendable.
Kuldip, by contrast, had to be grabbed intact. At least, I
hoped this was what their strategy was. If I was wrong,
Kuldip was going to be in deep trouble.

I wasn't too concerned about my own safety. People
might be watching windows and doors but nobody would
expect me to pop out of a skylight in the roof, even if they
knew it was there. Thackeray had laughed at me the
previous day when I'd spent a few minutes oiling the
hinges and catch. I hadn't minded at the time and I
minded even less now. No precaution was too small if it
might help to keep me alive.

The big danger was the moon. Fortunately there were
plenty of big black clouds scudding around in the night
sky, and I waited for one of the biggest of them to obscure
the moon before I slid out of the skylight. By the time the
moon had reappeared I was safely out of sight, crouching
behind the low parapet which ran round the roof.

Although I had a longish crawl ahead of me and there
was no way of managing this in total silence, the same

wind which was scudding the clouds about was doing a grand job of rustling the trees. Provided I didn't go mad and start heaving loose tiles over the parapet, nobody would be able to hear me. Nor, I hoped, would they see me coming down from the roof. One end of the chalet was blank wall, no windows, no doors, nothing apart from a drainpipe. Thackeray would have been able to enjoy another belly laugh at my expense if he'd seen me testing its strength after I'd finished oiling the skylight but I found it a considerable source of comfort to know it would bear my weight without pulling away from the wall. All I needed was another few seconds of darkness and as soon as I had it, I went straight over the parapet. I was working to a timetable and if Kuldip made her move before I was ready for her, we really would have problems.

Once I was in the trees the wind which had been so helpful while I was up on the roof, became something of a nuisance. Although it concealed any noise I might make padding through the woods, it would do the same for anybody else who was out and about. The very last thing I wanted was to trip over any hostile bodies while Kuldip was still inside the chalet. This was why I went fairly deep into the trees before I worked my way to the position I'd selected, more or less opposite the back door.

Kuldip's instinct for self-preservation was almost as highly developed as my own and she followed my instructions to the letter. She must have been nervous, all alone in the darkened building, and the moment the second-hand of her watch hit the mark I'd specified, she was out of the door and running. I hadn't mentioned anything about the moon or clouds and they weren't a consideration she took into account. Nobody could possibly have missed her when she came out of the door like a black thunderbolt, and she had an impressive running style. There was only about fifty yards of open ground between the house and the trees, and for the first twenty-five yards she was running at a tangent to me. Although she covered the ground fast, I knew I had at least two men to deal with before she reached the halfway point.

'Don't shoot.' The man spoke in French and he was frighteningly close to where I was. 'It's the woman.'

'I'll head her off.' The second voice was away to my left. 'You watch the house for the bastard with the shotgun.'

This was when Kuldip, still following instructions, abruptly changed course, cutting back towards where I was supposed to be. Although the voices would have startled her because I'd implied I was going out first to immobilize any opposition, she had the sense to realize I was her only hope. And, whatever doubts might be running through Kuldip's mind, it was working far better than I'd hoped. The man who'd spoken first couldn't believe his luck. Kuldip was going to run straight down his throat and he made the mistake of standing up to welcome her. By this time I'd already closed right up on him and it didn't even occur to him that there might be any danger threatening from behind. All of his attention was still beamed in on Kuldip when I let him have the butt of the shotgun in the back of his neck.

Nor did Kuldip turn her head when she went past. The second man was crashing through the trees after her, a couple of shouts from the front of the chalet suggested that reinforcements were on their way and she wasn't thinking about anything except running. She was no more than ten yards away from me as she weaved through the trees, heading uphill as I'd told her, and she had no idea I was there. I was the only one in the woods that night not making any noise and I only had a few seconds to wait before my second victim came crashing along in Kuldip's wake, cursing as the odd branch whipped back into his face. He wasn't any more at home in the woods than his companion had been and he had no chance to slam on the brakes when I suddenly materialized in front of him. In fact, it was his own forward momentum which did most of the damage when I jabbed him in the stomach with the muzzle of the shotgun. Still moving forward, he obligingly jackknifed over, giving me a clear shot at the nape of his neck with the butt.

In my original concept, this was the point where I should have disengaged and quietly faded away, following Kuldip up the hill. What I hadn't allowed for was the amount of noise one frightened Ugandan woman could make in a French forest at night. The wind had dropped, the steep slope was slowing Kuldip down and the noise she was making carried clearly to where I was standing. This meant it was also carrying to the men who had arrived from the front of the chalet. There were at least three of them and, as they weren't sure what was happening, they were being considerably more circumspect than their unconscious companions had been.

'Marc, Charles,' one of them called softly. 'What the hell is going on out there?'

Neither Marc nor Charles was in a position to answer but I decided to give them a subtle hint. Although there were too many trees in the way for me to have a hope of hitting anybody, they were going to be even more circumspect now they knew I was taking pot shots at them with the shotgun. The answering burst from a semi-automatic rifle encouraged me to be the same and I retreated a few yards uphill, selecting a new position behind a fallen tree trunk. It was only a short burst, no more than half a dozen rounds, before one of them realized Kuldip was somewhere in the woods as well and the shooting stopped.

For a minute or two nothing much happened except that the noise Kuldip was making grew gradually fainter. It didn't take the men below me very long to decide what

they had to do. I couldn't see them and I wasn't privy to
their discussion but they didn't have many alternatives.
Either they allowed us to escape or they split up and came
into the woods after me. There was never any real doubt
about what their decision would be and all I was waiting
for was for Kuldip to move out of earshot. Once I could
no longer hear her, I fired off a couple of random shots
and cleared out. I'd done my bit to guarantee that our
pursuers wouldn't be crowding us.

While I was much quieter than Kuldip had been, I was
also much faster because I knew precisely where I was going. She'd simply run uphill until she'd reached the
stream, then followed it, still going uphill, until she
reached the small waterfall. This was where I found her,
lurking in the shadows of a cluster of rocks, and I considered it advisable to announce myself before I stepped
into the open. Thackeray had equipped her with a little
MAB .25 automatic and I didn't want her doing any
target practice on me.
    'It's Philis,' I said quietly from the shelter of the trees.
'Don't shoot.'
    'I ought to, you bastard.' Kuldip was evidently grateful
for what I'd done for her. 'I thought I was supposed to
have a clear run from the chalet.'
    'Nobody stopped you, did they?' I pointed out, reason-
ably enough. 'In any case, this isn't the time or place for a
discussion. We have some walking to do.'
    After a quarter of an hour she didn't feel like talking at
all, let alone arguing with me. I set a pace fast enough to
make my own leg muscles come out with the odd protest
and she had to struggle to keep up with me. I suspected it
was pride which made her stay with me for as long as she
did. She hadn't forgiven me for her fright when she'd left
the chalet, and sheer bloody-mindedness made her determined to die before she admitted that she couldn't stand

the pace. However, even female bloody-mindedness had to have its limits.

'What's the rush for?' she panted at last. 'You said yourself that nobody could possibly follow us in the dark.'

'They couldn't.' I was talking over my shoulder. Kuldip had hoped I'd slow down to answer her, but I'd settled into a rhythm I was reluctant to break until this became absolutely necessary. 'Unfortunately, that's the least of our worries.'

Kuldip had slowed down and for the next few seconds she needed all her breath to catch up with me again.

'So why are we hurrying?'

'Because, unless they're absolute idiots, those men down there will have realized they're wasting their time blundering around in the dark. They'll have started wondering where, if anywhere, we're heading. If they happen to have a large-scale map of the area with them, they may be able to manage a very educated guess.'

This was the kind of reasoning Kuldip understood. For the next mile or so she gritted her teeth and struggled on but there had to come a time when willpower alone wasn't enough. As soon as I realized she couldn't keep up any longer, I slowed down myself. We'd made far better time than I'd anticipated and, if I did push Kuldip too hard, I'd end up having to carry her. The easier pace made talking more of a feasible proposition and I had a question of my own which I'd been saving for an appropriate occasion.

'Tell me something,' I said. 'Do many people in Uganda speak French?'

'No, of course they don't.' Kuldip sounded surprised by my question. 'English and Swahili are the two most common languages.'

'That's what I thought. How about Marc and Charles? Are they common names in Uganda?'

'Of course not. Nearly all the names are tribal.'

Although she must have been curious, Kuldip didn't have the energy to maintain the conversation any longer and I wasn't handing out gratuitous information. I reckoned she had enough to worry about already without me adding to her problems. I didn't believe in white French-speaking Ugandans any more than she did. Either some form of unholy alliance had been forged or a third group had entered the chase.

When we were still a couple of hundred yards from where I'd left the Datsun, I made Kuldip stop. I couldn't see how it could have been discovered by the opposition but I was way past the point where I was prepared to take anything on trust.

'Stay here,' I whispered. 'I'll flash the headlights if it's safe for you to join me.'

Kuldip was too tired to do more than nod her head and I guessed she was glad of the rest. I was tired, too, but this wasn't the reason I only spent a few seconds checking the area. It was far too dark for me to have a hope of finding anybody who didn't want to be found. The best I could do was leave Kuldip in relative safety and approach the Datsun from a direction diametrically opposed to the one where she was hidden. If the worst should have happened, at least we wouldn't have all our eggs in the one basket.

Nobody shot me and there was no explosion when I switched on the ignition and this was all the reassurance I was likely to get. Once I was safely on the track, I flashed the headlights and sat behind the wheel until Kuldip joined me, ready to take off in the best Le Mans style at the slightest sign of interference. Driving down the track without either head- or sidelights was a slow and awkward process. It was also necessary because until I knew precisely what we were up against I had to be a pessimist and assume the worst. For the last downhill section before the track reached the surfaced road I switched off the engine and coasted. While we were still a good hundred yards away, I pulled in under the trees.

'What are you doing?' Kuldip asked.

Until this point she hadn't really questioned anything I'd done and she wasn't now. It was simply that the tension was beginning to tell. She knew as well as I did that the road signalled the start of the real danger area because there would be cars out looking for us.

'I'm going to take a quick look ahead,' I told her. 'You'd better move over into the driving seat. If I should run into any trouble, get the hell out of here as fast as you can.'

'What about you?'

Kuldip wasn't worried about me. She just didn't want to be left on her own.

'I'll make out,' I said. 'Besides, I'm being paid to take the risks.'

I'd also be considerably safer on my own but I didn't want to detract from my noble sentiments by saying so. Once again, it was impossible to check properly but I went along the road for a short distance in both directions without encountering anything at all suspicious. On the way back to Kuldip I tried to decide what to do next, a decision which would have been considerably easier to reach if I hadn't been operating in a vacuum. While we'd been avoiding a bunch of Ugandans it had all been relatively straightforward. They were as easy to identify as Kuldip herself and their manpower was limited. Now they seemed to have acquired some local help and nothing was straightforward any more. I was no longer even sure who or what we were running away from. The only real certainty was that I'd end up like Thackeray if I allowed myself to be caught.

'Is everything OK?' Kuldip enquired as I resumed my seat behind the wheel.

'It seems to be.'

'What's our next move, then?'

'I think we stick to the route I worked out with Thackeray.' I hadn't been sure of my answer until I'd actually said it. 'It's still our best bet for reaching the boat safely.'

There were a few seconds' silence while Kuldip considered my reply. She was no fool and she could read a map so it didn't take her long to come up with her next question.

'Doesn't that mean driving back past the chalet?'

'It needn't do,' I admitted as I switched on the ignition, 'but that was the way I was thinking of going. It's nothing to worry about, though. That's the last road anybody will be expecting us to use.'

'So you say.' Although Kuldip wasn't arguing, she didn't sound particularly confident. 'I hope you know what you're doing.'

So did I, but I wasn't about to share any of my doubts. Our real troubles were likely to arrive with daylight.

NICE, FRANCE

Ferrier was finished. The decision was irrevocable, regardless of whether they caught up with the woman again or not, and it had been reached the moment Martel had heard the gunfire. His Citroën had been about to turn into the driveway and the driver had needed no instructions about what to do in such a situation. He'd gone straight past, heading away from the chalet, and taken Martel back to Nice. The days when Martel had used a gun were long since past.

Nothing Martel had heard since he'd been back at the villa had tempted him to change his mind about Ferrier. However, this was something to be settled in the future.

Martel prided himself on being a pragmatist and for the time being he still needed Ferrier's assistance. This was why he masked his hostility when Ferrier arrived, although he made no secret of his displeasure.

'Well?' Martel demanded.

'The woman and one of her bodyguards escaped.'

Ferrier's tone was defiant. He knew he was entirely to blame for the fiasco but this wasn't something he was prepared to admit to anybody else.

'So I gathered, but that wasn't what I meant. How much attention did the shooting attract?'

'None, so far as I know.' Ferrier felt relieved. The older man wasn't creating as much of a scene as he'd expected. 'We pulled out pretty fast once we realized they were clear but we took the time to tidy up a little before we left.'

'How many casualties were there?'

'Two, one of mine and one of theirs. We didn't dare bring the bodies with us so they're still in the garage at the chalet. If it's clear in the morning, I'll send out a couple of men to shift them.'

'Pick one man and Paul can go with him. After all, this is supposed to be a joint venture.' Martel paused a second to allow the barb to sink home. 'More important, do you have any idea where the woman might have gone?'

'Well, I'd say they must have had an escape route ready prepared.' Ferrier was anxious to redeem himself and this was the only hope he had. 'They probably had a car stashed over the other side of the mountain. There are plenty of places they could have left it. Anyway, it doesn't matter too much. I found this on the man we killed.'

Although the sheet of paper was bloodstained, most of the writing was clearly legible. Martel knew the area well enough to see that the towns and villages listed on it traced an intricate route to the north, designed to avoid most of the main population centres. It seemed as though Ferrier's stupidity needn't necessarily be as disastrous as

Martel had first feared.

Nor could he find anything to criticize in the arrangements Ferrier had made. He'd used the radio-telephone in his car to ensure all the roads to the north were covered and he'd even had the sense not to neglect likely routes to the east and west. This wouldn't be sufficient to save him but for the time being it was satisfactory enough. If the woman was still in the area, she'd be effectively bottled up. If she wasn't, Martel now knew where she was going and it would only take a phone call or two to extend the search area. Fifty million francs' worth of rubies wasn't a prize Martel was prepared to concede easily.

CHAPTER 9

When the first car flashed its headlights at me I didn't pay a great deal of attention. After a second driver had done the same, I did. I was driving on the correct side of the road, my own headlights were dipped and I was obeying as much of the French highway code as I could remember so there was only one reason for the signals that I could think of. The international cameraderie of the road was at work, if I was right. It was one of those magic moments when, in the face of a common enemy, drivers stopped trying to force one another off the road and spared a thought for other road users. Kuldip hadn't seen the flashing headlights because she'd been dozing, but she did notice when I pulled on to the verge.

'Oh Christ,' she said unenthusiastically. 'There's no need to tell me. I wait here in the car while you take a look ahead.'

This was just the kind of remark I needed to encourage me. It gave me a warm glow inside to know my efforts to keep her alive and well were appreciated.

'Not this time,' I told her. 'It's your turn to stretch your legs. Take a quick tour round the car and make sure all the lights are working.'

Although she still wasn't looking particularly enthusiastic, I was coming to recognize Kuldip's petulance as an integral part of her nature. She was one of those people who was automatically prejudiced against any suggestion which wasn't her own. It only took her a few seconds to check up on the Datsun's circuitry, then she was back in the car.

'It all looks OK to me,' she reported. 'What now?'

'We revert to plan A. You wait in the car while I take a look ahead. I shouldn't be too long.'

Until I rounded the second bend in the road I wasn't sure what I was looking for. The flashing headlights had made me think of the police but policemen came in many forms. The ones we had to cope with had established a road block of sorts. They'd parked their vehicle beside the road and were using their flashlights to flag down those motorists who interested them. I hung around for a couple of minutes, just to confirm that they really were only interested in northbound traffic. Then I headed back to Kuldip and the Datsun.

'Well?' she enquired.

'There's a police road block up ahead.'

'For us?'

When she was frightened, Kuldip forgot all about being petulant.

'That is the sixty-four-thousand-dollar question,' I admitted. 'I can't really be sure.'

I had no such doubts about what we had to do. Whatever the reasons for the late night, or early morning, police activity, we had to behave as though it was aimed at us. The road block was too much of a coincidence for us to do anything else.

Coincidence or not, something had occurred to me that

I should have thought of before. When I first put the question to her Kuldip wasn't co-operative.

'How would I know?' she demanded. 'You and Thackeray sorted it out between you. Both of you made it perfectly clear that I was only the passenger.'

'I know, I know.' This was too important for me to waste time humouring Kuldip. 'You were too busy doing your fingernails to pay any attention to what we were saying. That isn't what I'm asking. He wrote the route down on a piece of paper. I'm trying to establish exactly what he did with the paper.'

At first Kuldip said she didn't know, but I kept nagging away at her and at last she decided Thackeray might have put the piece of paper in his pocket. Although she didn't want to commit herself, this was what she thought he'd done with it. I thought so too. If we were correct, this gave us a very good reason for changing our itinerary, regardless of the road block. The chances were that all the other roads north would be equally dangerous and I'd had more than enough for one night. Before I made another attempt for northern France and the boat, I needed to know precisely what we were up against.

Whatever its other virtues, the Datsun was no mobile home. Its designers hadn't intended it to be used as a dormitory. In any case, I didn't want to run the risk of being caught in the open. The alternative had its risks but these weren't nearly as great as Kuldip thought they were when she realized where we were going. To begin with she was quite pleasantly surprised when I took her with me after I'd hidden the car in the woods. All she knew was that I had somewhere lined up for us to lie low and sleep for a few hours. It wasn't until she caught a glimpse of the chalet through the trees that she began to raise objections.

'Relax,' I told her. 'This is by far the safest place for us to be.'

'You're crazy, Philis.' Like me, she was talking in a whisper which I hoped wasn't necessary. 'They might still be here.'

'There's no chance of that. There's nothing for them here now they know we've gone.'

'What about the police?'

Kuldip wasn't getting any happier.

'What about them?' I countered. 'We didn't go running to them for help, did we? You can bet that the men who shot Thackeray didn't go to them either, not unless they fancied facing a murder charge.'

'There was a lot of shooting,' Kuldip persisted. 'Somebody could have heard it.'

'That's the best reason the opposition would have had for clearing out quickly. They couldn't risk being caught with any corpses on their hands. And, just in case you're wondering, the French police don't work in the dark. If they had been called in, we'd have known about it long before now.'

Calming Kuldip's fears was one thing, calming my own quite another. I thought I was right. I thought the chalet was far and away the safest place for us to be over the next few hours but I'd been wrong often enough in the past not to take my logic for granted. Everything looked normal enough. The camper had been extricated from the trees and pushed back into the garage. Although I looked, I couldn't find any bodies littering the woods. On the surface it seemed as though the opposition had done what I'd hoped they'd do. After they'd failed to grab us, they'd done a bit of tidying up and gone off to make their plans for trapping us before we escaped the area. The police I could discount completely, despite the inexplicable road block. If they were coming to the chalet, if a neighbour or passing motorist had heard the shooting and phoned in, they'd have been there already.

Our major safety factor had been touched on by

Kuldip when she'd said I must be crazy to think of returning to the chalet. It was an attitude I was relying on. We were supposed to be on the run. We should be putting as much distance as possible between us and the one place we'd been pinpointed, not strolling back into the lions' den. This was what people should be thinking but I couldn't rely on everybody being as logical as I was. The acid test of my theorizing would come when Kuldip and I emerged into the open and went into the chalet.

'Remember,' I said to Kuldip. 'Keep behind me. At the first hint of trouble clear out fast and head back to the Datsun.'

'Thanks for nothing,' Kuldip whispered back. 'That's what I'd decided to do anyway.'

It was rather anticlimactic to discover my soul-searching hadn't been necessary. Although we couldn't afford to switch on the lights, there was nothing to indicate that anybody had been inside the chalet since our hurried departure. However, I wasn't quite finished, even after I'd made a quick check of all the rooms. There was something else I wanted to look at.

Residual gallantry made me suggest to Kuldip that she might prefer to stay in the house while I went to the garage but my suggestion wasn't appreciated. She didn't want to be left on her own in the dark. When I pointed out that what I expected to find wouldn't be very pleasant, Kuldip simply shrugged and said it couldn't possibly be any worse than some of the things she'd witnessed before she'd left Uganda. After this I didn't bother to argue any more.

When I opened the back of the camper, the big surprise was that there were two bodies inside, not one. Even so, I concentrated on Thackeray first. Ever since I'd jumped out of the camper to do my cowboy bit in the drive, I'd been aware of the faint possibility that he might still have been alive. I only had to look at the state of his head in the light of the pencil flash to realize I needn't have worried. He would have died instantaneously, and even Kuldip managed a sharp intake of breath. The discovery didn't do anything to ease my conscience, mainly because I hadn't been suffering any pangs of guilt to start with. Under the circumstances, I wouldn't have stayed to lend him a helping hand even if I'd been positive he was still alive. Nevertheless, I was glad to know Thackeray couldn't have suffered a great deal. I was almost equally glad to know that he couldn't have spoken to anybody before he died. The opposition seemed to know too many of our plans as it was.

The second body belonged to the man I'd caught with the shotgun. Although he was just as dead, he wasn't in nearly as bad a condition as Thackeray, and I spent a few seconds going through his pockets. It was an unprofitable exercise because somebody had done the same job before me. All I learned was that he wasn't Ugandan and he bought his clothes in Nice. Once I'd closed the door of the camper on the corpses, I decided it was way past my bedtime.

'What about the bodies?' Kuldip asked when I'd said what I intended to do.

'They're safe enough where they are.'

'You're just going to leave them?'

'Why not? They're not going to run away before the morning.'

They weren't going to run away even then and I'd no intention of digging any graves. Unless I was very much mistaken, somebody should be coming to the chalet to dispose of them for us.

One or other of us should really have kept watch for the remainder of the night but it was a question of priorities. In the end I contented myself with one or two rudimentary devices which would give us some warning of unwel-

come visitors and left it at that. Neither of us could function without sleep and there was no telling when we'd
next be able to rest.

In any case, I didn't think we would be disturbed. Contrary to popular fallacy, the small hours of the morning
aren't the time to ferry corpses around the countryside,
and even a quiet burial in the woods isn't something to be
rushed. Somewhere or other, people would be paying
close attention to the news and the newspaper headlines.
Other people would be making periodic trips past the
bottom of the drive, checking for signs of police activity at
the chalet. Although they'd need to dispose of the
evidence, they'd only do so when they were sure they were
safe.

It helped to know I must be up against some kind of
professional organization. Amateurs would have considered it a risk to leave the bodies behind. Only people
who had done it before would realize that the killing was
the easy part. It was the disposal operation which took the
most care and planning.

Although I didn't have too many qualms about dragging Kuldip off to bed, sleeping with her wasn't nearly as
exciting as I'd imagined it might be. It was a let-down
which probably had something to do with the separate
beds. Common sense might dictate that we both use the
bedroom I'd previously shared with Thackeray but there
were no sexual undertones at all. We'd both been through
too much for that. We simply pulled our clothes off in the
dark, said good night and tumbled into bed. I must have
fallen asleep while my head was still a couple of inches
above the pillow.

Tired or not, the mental alarm clock inside my head
only allowed me four hours. When I unwillingly dragged
myself back to consciousness, Kuldip was still out, lips
slightly apart, black hair spread over the pillow. In sleep
she acquired an innocence and vulnerability which wasn't

normally apparent and I thought what a shame it would
be to disturb her. This was a fraction of a second before I
lobbed the spare pillow at her. She was awake instantly,
nostrils flared as though she scented danger.

'What's the matter?'

'It's breakfast time. I've just unanimously voted you
cook.'

Although she grimaced, it was too early in the day for
petulance. Her only objection was half-hearted.

'I'm not wearing anything,' she said.

'I know.'

This was something I'd thought of before I'd thrown
the pillow at her. With a lousy job like mine, I needed a
few fringe benefits.

'If you were a gentleman,' she said, throwing back the
covers, 'you'd turn your head while I get out of bed.'

I'd always known my lack of breeding would pay
dividends some time. In any case, Kuldip was an exhi-
bitionist at heart. It was women with sagging breasts,
stretch marks and jodhpur thighs who were shy. The
lucky few, like Kuldip, were only too glad of an appreciative audience. She made getting dressed a hell of a
sight more entertaining than most of the strip shows I'd
seen.

'I hope you've been eating your heart out,' she said
when she'd finished with the zipper on her jeans.

'It's not my heart you have to worry about,' I told her.

At least she was laughing as she set off for the kitchen. I
didn't think she'd find a lot more to amuse her during the
rest of the day.

I assumed the disposal unit would be working normal
office hours, which meant they shouldn't arrive before
nine at the earliest. This gave us plenty of time for a
leisurely breakfast, cooked as badly as only Kuldip knew
how. The blinds on the windows meant we could move

freely about the chalet and we took our coffee through to the living-room to escape the smell of scorched frying-pan.

'When are we leaving?' Kuldip asked. 'Are we waiting for nightfall?'

'I doubt it,' I answered. 'We'll probably have some company before then.'

'Company?'

Kuldip was startled. She was gradually becoming accustomed to the idea that the chalet really might be the safest place for us to be and I'd just shattered her illusions.

'That's what I said. Don't worry about it, though. We'll be ready for them.'

Long before I'd finished explaining what I thought would happen, Kuldip had reverted to a familiar theme, maintaining I must be crazy. I only succeeded in reinforcing this opinion when I proceeded to explain what I intended to do. In fact, she used some forceful and most unladylike language to suggest we leave the chalet immediately. It was an argument which ended when I told Kuldip I was staying but she was at perfect liberty to go any time she wanted to. After this, she contented herself with the odd glower and mutter. Fortunately, she didn't have very long to develop her bad temper. The telephone started ringing at about half past nine and this gave her something else to think about.

'The telephone is ringing,' she said observantly.

'Well, I never.' Sarcasm was my forte. 'I wondered what the noise could be.'

I was sitting by one of the windows where I commanded a good view of the drive. Until the telephone rang I'd been wondering whether the disposal unit might be a figment of my imagination. Now I no longer had any such doubts.

'Who do you think it is?'

'It could be the telephone company checking to see if they've repaired the lines properly,' I said. 'I don't think it is, though. I'd say it's somebody who's hoping there won't be any answer. Our company should be arriving soon.'

They weren't in any rush. They'd read the newspapers, they'd listened to the news, they'd driven slowly past the chalet and they'd even gone to the bother of reconnecting the phone but there was always an outside chance they might have rung the wrong number. Five minutes later the telephone started ringing again. This time Kuldip didn't state the obvious. Instead she looked across to me for reassurance and I responded with a smile. Although she'd shown far more resilience than I could have expected, the strain was beginning to tell.

'I do know what I'm doing,' I told her. 'This is what I was hired for.'

Kuldip didn't actually have her fingers crossed but she looked as if she might be reserving judgment.

The van had *Electricité de France* plastered all over it and both the men inside wore appropriately mono-grammed overalls. They probably even had their bags of tools in the back. Although they parked in front of the garage, backing up so they were only a few feet from the door, they didn't simply jump out and start transferring the bodies. They'd established a cover of sorts and they intended to play it straight until they were positive the precaution was unnecessary.

As they strolled towards the front door, I tried to size them up. What I saw wasn't particularly encouraging. Neither of them was really big but they both looked hard and durable. Worse still, they looked very competent. They were moving unhurriedly, casually chatting together as they walked, doing a job of work they'd un-doubtedly done before. I couldn't even derive a great deal of satisfaction from the fact that one of them was young,

in his mid-twenties. The criminal classes along the
Riviera grew up fast or they didn't grow up at all.

'What are they doing?' Kuldip whispered in my ear.

Under other circumstances I would have considered the
breast pressing against my arm to be a provocation. Now
I knew Kuldip was nervous, standing as close as she could
for comfort.

'They've come to read the meter,' I told her. 'If anybody is at home, they've come to ask permission.'

They played the doorbell routine as coolly as they'd
played everything else. After they'd rung, they stood on
the top step and continued their conversation. I couldn't
hear the actual words but it sounded natural enough. A
few seconds later they rang the bell again. Then when
nobody answered, they turned away, heading back
towards the garage as unhurriedly as they'd come.

'Right,' I said to Kuldip. 'You know what to do.'

She nodded nervously before going across to the table
and picking up the roll of insulating tape I'd dug out of
one of the cupboards.

'I'll call you when I'm ready,' I told her. 'Until then
keep out of sight.'

Repeating the instructions was a sign that my own
adrenalin was flowing. It seemed an awful long time since
I'd last taken the initiative.

LONDON, ENGLAND

Richard Montgomery was head of the African Section, a
big, raw-boned man with a shock of bristly, red hair
which was an accurate reflection of his temper. Even
when he was on his best behaviour he had an abrasive
manner and he always managed to look as though he was
engaged in a permanent vendetta with his clothes. None

of this stopped him from being very good at his work.

'It looks as though you're right, sir.'

The 'sir' was tacked on as an afterthought. Montgomery's respect for Pawson didn't mean that he automatically conceded him superiority.

'You're sure of that?'

'As sure as I can be without a sworn affidavit. We can
definitely place her a few miles from the Franco-Italian
border the day Philis flew out.'

'I see.' Pawson sounded smug. There was nothing he
enjoyed more than being proved right. 'The only question
is, would she have had access to the information we think
she did?'

'There's no doubt of that. None at all. As I told you
before, she did a hell of a lot more than keep Amin's bed
warm for him. That's why she lasted so long. For the last
couple of years she doubled up as mistress and a very
special private assistant. There's no way of checking, of
course, but I can't see anybody else making the travel
arrangements. I'd put money on it.'

This was as good as a personal guarantee. Montgomery
didn't commit himself lightly.

'How about the other list?' Pawson enquired. 'That's
the one which interests me. And Sir Keith Tenby, come to
that.'

'If it does exist, she'd know about it. I think there has to
be documentary evidence of some kind. Amin had his
sane moments and he knew all about using levers. Tenby
must believe in its existence, otherwise he wouldn't be
putting all this effort into bringing her to England.'

'There are the rubies as well. They'd make for quite an
incentive.'

Pawson didn't believe this for a moment. He was simply
prodding Montgomery.

'I don't think she has them, not the bulk of them,
anyway.' Montgomery was dogmatic about this. 'The way

I read the situation, she was used as a courier to take them out of Uganda. Then, when the split was made, she got the short end of the stick. It's the only reason I can think of for her making waves. If she had the rubies she wouldn't need Tenby's help, or anybody else's. She's more than capable of looking after herself.'

Pawson nodded thoughtfully, allowing himself a small smile of satisfaction. He liked the way the picture was shaping.

'What about Philis?' Montgomery asked suddenly. 'Are you going to give him a fuller briefing?'

'I'm not in contact with him at the moment.'

Now it was Montgomery's turn to smile.

'And if you were?'

'Who knows?'

They both knew Pawson wasn't being honest. However much he might protest to the contrary, Philis functioned best when he was convinced everybody's hand was turned against him.

CHAPTER 10

When I stepped into the garage, one body was already in the back of the electricity van and Thackeray's corpse was on its way to join it. I was holding my Colt Python where nobody could possibly miss it. A .357 Magnum is the kind of weapon which commands a lot of respect from people who know anything about handguns and the two French-men stopped what they were doing as soon as they saw me. They would have probably dumped Thackeray on the oil-stained concrete if I hadn't forestalled them.

'Stay exactly where you are.' Although my French might not be particularly fluent, neither man was going to bother about my accent while I had the gun. 'Mr

Thackeray was a friend of mine. I'd be very angry if you didn't handle him with a little respect.'

Both men decided they didn't want me to be angry, although the younger of the two took a fraction of a second longer to make up his mind than his companion. The two of them stood where they were, supporting Thackeray's dead weight, and wondering what came next. As they knew who I must be, they couldn't have had too many illusions.

'Now,' I said. 'Let's see how good a sense of balance you have. Use your left hands to unbutton the front of your overalls. There's no hurry, so take it nice and easy.'

Balancing the body took too much of their attention for them to consider any heroics. Besides, they only had to glance down at what they were holding to see what guns could do and this wouldn't have encouraged them. Once the overalls were unbuttoned, I made them remove their own weapons one at a time, taking the younger man first. This was another manoeuvre they had to perform left-handed and I made it perfectly clear that thumbs and forefingers were the order of the day. It was a routine both men understood.

'Fine,' I told them. 'Load the body into the back of the van, then lie down on the floor.'

So far neither of the Frenchmen had spoken. They were far too busy thinking, hunting around for a way out. There wasn't one, not unless they wanted to be shot, which was why they ended up on the floor. When they were there, the older man at last tried a question.

'What do you want?' he asked.

Although he wasn't being at all original, there was no mistaking his interest in my answer.

'All in good time,' I said. 'Let's get you two tidied up first. Roll over on to your stomachs and put your hands behind your backs.'

Once they were in position, I moved away from the

doorway for the first time, going across to kick the discarded automatics under the camper where they'd no longer be such a temptation. Only then did I call for Kuldip to join me. I'd already briefed her on what to do with the insulation tape and she made a thorough job of it. There weren't any knots for them to work at so the men's wrists were going to stay taped together until somebody decided to release them.

After she'd finished we passed an entertaining few seconds watching the Frenchmen learn how to push themselves up on to their feet with their chins, a process they didn't find nearly as amusing as Kuldip did. They were even less amused when we'd gone inside the chalet and they were split up. The younger man went with me into the bedroom while his companion stayed with Kuldip. She had the shotgun to lend her a little authority and I didn't have any doubts at all about her being prepared to use it.

My choice of prisoners wasn't completely arbitrary. There were any number of factors which made it imperative for me to work fast. I had to dig out what information I could as quickly as I could and there was no time for subtlety. I had to establish my credentials with a minimum of fuss and this was why I'd selected the younger man. He was good-looking in a dark, greasy sort of way and, to anybody who knew what he was looking for, he had the unmistakable mark of the street on him. He was tough and he was probably ambitious and he wasn't going to answer my questions simply because I asked him nicely. Given the time, breaking him wouldn't have been a problem but I didn't intend to bother. He was simply the lever I was going to use to persuade the other man to co-operate.

He was everything I'd expected him to be. Although he was intelligent enough to be frightened by what might happen to him, fear sparked defiance and aggression. He

automatically dropped into a role which must have been
culled from a diet of second-rate movie and TV thrillers.
He wasn't going to tell me a thing no matter what I did to
him. He cast himself as the hero of his own private fantasy
and he wouldn't even tell me his name. He did come out
with a few obscenities which did wonders for my grasp of
colloquial French but this was all. I responded in the way
he obviously expected and knocked him about a bit.
While I hurt him enough to make him yell once or twice,
I was simply going through the motions and he'd never
realize how lightly he'd escaped. Slaps sounded far more
spectacular than punches and, as my main interest was in
audience response, I only used my open hand. When he
fell it was because I'd pushed him, not because I'd hit him
particularly hard. To the man next door it would sound
as though I was beating the living daylights out of him
and this was the illusion I was endeavouring to create.

It was all rather tedious and after five minutes or so I
decided the charade had lasted long enough. When I
used the barrel of the Python on his head, I did hit him
hard and he went down with a most satisfactory crash,
taking most of the contents of the dressing table with him.

Although I didn't normally waste my time talking to
people who couldn't hear me, this was an exception and I
deliberately raised my voice while I finished my arrangements. The dialogue was corny, consisting of a 'This is
your last chance' theme, but it helped to fill in an
awkward gap. The bottle of tomato ketchup was already
in the bedroom and as I spoke I tastefully arranged liberal
quantities on the back of the unconscious man's head and
the carpet beneath it. This might be a ploy which was
even cornier than my monologue but it wasn't intended to
withstand close scrutiny. The bottle went under the bed,
then I pulled back the covers and fired twice into the mattress, holding the Python far enough away to make sure I
didn't burn the house down. With the covers back in

place, my illusion was complete.

As I'd had my doubts about Kuldip's acting ability, I hadn't warned her what to expect. Consequently she looked as stunned as our second prisoner when I appeared in the bedroom doorway. They'd heard murder being committed and admiration wasn't the dominant expression on either face. The reaction encouraged me to ham it up a bit more, working to maintain my new-found stature.

'You,' I said, talking to the man on the floor. 'Come over here.'

He came, just as fast as he could. I helped him on his way with a shove which sent him careering into the door-jamb.

'Take a good look at your friend,' I suggested. 'I want you to realize I'm not playing games.'

The moral of my little sermon wasn't wasted on him. When he looked away I knew I had him. He wanted to live long enough to draw his old-age pension.

Paul had the look of a street-corner Charles Aznavour and he'd been around long enough to have earned the grey hairs which were taking over his sideburns. He was almost certain I was going to kill him whether he co-operated or not, but 'almost' was a very important word. After what he thought he'd seen in the bedroom, he knew for a fact that I'd kill him if he didn't co-operate. Like most people, he was a devout believer in the old adage about life being equated to hope. This was the attitude I'd been trying to encourage and I hoped Paul had taken his thinking a stage further. He had absolutely no idea how much I knew already and, hopefully, this should encourage him not to feed me too many lies.

What he had to say certainly had the ring of truth about it, even to the extent that there were some areas about which he knew nothing at all. As Paul was no more than the hired help, I'd have been instantly suspicious if

he'd had an answer for everything. Despite these unavoid-
able gaps, he told me more than enough to explain what
had been happening, especially as I was in a position to
fill in several of the missing pieces myself.

The shame of it was that Thackeray's decoy seemed to
have done her job. She had driven to Marseilles without
arousing any suspicions and she had successfully ditched
her tail. It had been left to the Ugandans to cock everything up for us. In a demographic sense Marseilles was a
large city, with a metropolitan population of over a
million. However, in a criminal sense it was strictly
parochial, with both the police and their prey operating
within clearly defined limits. One Ugandan wandering
around and asking questions would have attracted little
more than passing curiosity. With several of them all doing the same thing it had been virtually inevitable that
sooner or later somebody would want to find out why. It
could easily have been the police who had stepped in first
but, in the event, it had been Paul's boss, Louis Martel,
who had made the move.

His orders had been to pick up one of the Ugandans
and squeeze him a little until he'd explained what he and
his friends were doing. Although Paul hadn't been a
party to what had happened next, it was obvious what
had taken place. The Ugandan had talked, and mention
of a few million francs' worth of rubies had struck a
responsive chord somewhere deep inside Martel. It
wouldn't have taken him long to decide to go looking for
the lady himself and, apparently, he'd soon been successful.

From what Paul told me, Martel was the big man in
Marseilles, a cross between the Godfather and Al Capone,
but I wasn't sure how accurate a description this was.
Despite all the literature on the subject, organized crime
was a media myth. As James Burke had proved in his
Connections, facts could be used to show what you

wanted them to show. The underworld was a reflection of the society it fed upon, with everybody looking out for himself. The concept of unswerving loyalty to a supreme criminal chief was no more realistic than expecting the average Englishman to lay down his life for Maggie Thatcher. As they had to live side by side, with the police as a common enemy, there had to be a degree of collaboration between the various factions but self-interest still reigned supreme.

Martel had had no doubts about where his interests lay and it must have come as a considerable shock to him to discover that the woman everybody had been hunting was no more than a decoy. Even so, he'd persevered. The decoy had given him Armand's phone number in Nice and this had been the point where the collaboration had come in. While Martel and his entourage, which had included Paul, had been travelling from Marseilles, contacts in Nice had been having a heart-to-heart with Armand. He had told them that Kuldip was still holed up somewhere in the area and from there on it had been a process of elimination, culminating in the attack on the chalet the previous night.

Although a lot of this was necessarily surmise, I now had a fair idea of what must have happened. A more accurate appraisal of the threat posed by Martel would have to wait until I'd been in touch with Pawson. What I had to do now, provided Kuldip could remember her lines, was spread some calculated misinformation.

'Exactly what happened after we escaped last night?' I asked.

'Like I said, I wasn't here, but I gather they cleared out.' Paul remained convinced that it was in his own best interests to co-operate and, where he had them, the answers were coming promptly. 'Once Ferrier realized you were off and running, he tidied up a little and then pulled out. With all the shooting he was afraid the police might turn up.'

'But Martel hasn't given up?'

'No way. Louis thought he had a rough idea which direction you were heading in and he called up some more local help. He's trying to cover all the most likely escape routes.'

'How about the police? Does Martel have a pull with them as well?'

'What do you mean?'

Paul was looking genuinely puzzled.

'There were police road blocks out last night. Were they anything to do with Martel?'

'Nothing at all.' Paul was sounding relieved. 'There was a big jewel heist in Cannes last night.'

I nodded. This fitted in with what I'd been thinking since I'd listened to the local news on the radio.

'What's the situation now? I take it there are still people out and about.'

It was Paul's turn to nod.

'Louis is sure you're still somewhere in the area. He's widened the circle a little but there are still people watching.'

'How about the borders?' Kuldip asked. I shot her a warning glance which she ignored but Paul didn't miss. 'Are they covered as well?'

'I really don't know.' Paul managed to sound suitably apologetic. 'I wasn't told the actual dispositions.'

Although I pressed him a bit more, I'd just about squeezed him dry. He was positive that the main roads must be covered but this was as far as he was prepared to commit himself. However, the questions weren't a complete waste of time. They allowed Kuldip an opportunity to make the other two contributions we'd rehearsed and both of them reinforced the impression she'd given earlier. When the time came, Paul should be telling people we were heading for the Swiss or Italian frontiers. If this bait was swallowed, it could make things considerably easier for us.

'One last question,' I said. 'What are the standing orders if we should be caught?'

'I don't understand.'

Paul understood perfectly but this was one question he didn't want to answer. His situation was precarious enough without him provoking me.

'Come on,' I said. 'Martel must have given some instructions about what to do if anybody should bump into us. I want to know what they are.'

When Paul did answer me the instructions proved to be pretty much what I'd expected. Kuldip wasn't to be harmed under any circumstances. She had to be recovered intact. I, on the other hand, was expendable. This was all the encouragement I needed to make sure I was even more careful than usual when we left the chalet.

NEAR GATTIÈRES, FRANCE

Even after the man and woman had gone, after he'd heard the door bang closed behind them, Paul suspected a trick. From the moment of his capture in the garage he'd known how it was going to end and Albert's death had merely confirmed his conviction. Just like him he'd finish with a bullet in the back of the head, no matter how co-operative he was. The most Paul had hoped for was to avoid being knocked around too much.

It was a full quarter of an hour before he realized that he might really have been reprieved and he began to consider how he could free himself. It took him almost ten minutes to worm his way through into the kitchen and another twenty with a knife before he'd cut through the tape on his wrists and ankles. All the same, Paul was glad they'd used tape. It hadn't cut off his circulation the way rope or wire would have done.

The next step was to telephone Martel and Paul had his story ready. He actually had the receiver in his hand when a noise from the back of the house stopped him. For a long second he stayed where he was, the sharp kitchen knife gripped in his free hand. Then he heard the noise again and this time he correctly identified it. They hadn't returned to deal with him but the alternative was almost as bad.

'Oh shit,' he said out loud. 'The lousy bastard.'

Although he had hardly moved from where Paul had last seen him, Albert was on the verge of consciousness. The blood which had previously looked so convincing when he'd been standing in the doorway smelled and tasted of ketchup now he was closer. Swearing under his breath, Paul helped Albert up on to the bed without smearing too much of the sauce on his overalls and started working on him, trying to bring him round. Carrying him out to the van was strictly a last resort. Slapping his face didn't do much good apart from making him groan a little but Paul had better luck with a jug of water from the bathroom.

'Come on, Albert,' he said, hauling him into a sitting position. 'We have to get out of here.'

'Telephone,' Albert mumbled. 'Must telephone Ferrier.'

He wasn't really conscious yet but some parts of his brain had started to function again.

'Not now. There isn't time.' Paul deliberately injected some urgency into his voice. 'The police may be on their way.'

These were the magic words which had Albert on his feet and stumbling towards the garage. Although Paul still had to support him, Albert seemed more aware of his surroundings by the time they reached the van. He was certainly aware enough not to want to go in the back with the two bodies.

'You can't possibly drive around the countryside smothered in tomato ketchup,' Paul explained patiently. 'That would be a sure way of attracting attention.'

Reluctantly Albert accepted the logic of this and allowed Paul to help him into the back. Once he was safely wedged against the side, there was only one thing left for Paul to do.

'I'll get our guns,' he said. 'Then we'd better start moving. Martel and Ferrier will be wondering what happened to us.'

Paul had known what he had to do from the moment he'd realized Albert was still alive, and he did it with a minimum of fuss, shooting Albert twice in the head before he had any idea he was about to die. Now Paul was covered. There would be nobody to pinpoint the inconsistencies and inaccuracies in the story he'd fabricated. He wouldn't have to mention the confidences he'd betrayed.

All Martel would be interested in was the information Paul had to give him. Like most women, the African bitch hadn't known when to keep her mouth closed and Paul hadn't been too scared to miss the slips she'd made. They'd be heading east, towards the Swiss or Italian frontiers, not north as Martel had imagined and they'd be travelling in a Citroën of some description. This should be more than enough to guarantee that Paul came out of the whole affair smelling of roses, and three bodies were as easy to dispose of as two.

CHAPTER 11

I'd had it up to the back teeth with the Riviera. The tourists were welcome to the beaches, bosoms and bars, but Philis wanted out. The longer I stayed cooped up be-

tween the Alps and the Mediterranean the more paranoid
I became. Now I had a better idea of what I was up
against, I wanted to be out in the open, somewhere I'd
have a bit more room for manoeuvre.

We made pretty good time the first day and by late
afternoon we'd reached Avignon. Once we'd left the
Rhône and the Palace of the Popes behind us, I finally
relented and allowed Kuldip out from under her blanket
in the back. This was a decision which had nothing at all
to do with her constant barrage of complaints. We needed
petrol and Kuldip would attract less attention sitting
beside me than she would huddled on the back seat.
When we'd filled up the tank and were on our way again,
she was in the mood for conversation.

'Are they the Causses?' she asked.

She was indicating the hills ahead of us.

'No, not yet.'

The Causses were where I intended to lose us for a
couple of days. As I'd explained, Martel and his cronies
were city slickers and they wouldn't have many contacts
where we were headed. If I remembered correctly, there
wasn't much to rob there apart from the sheep.

'How much further are they?'

'Quite a few miles the way we're going. We'll head
north for a while before we loop back. Anyway, that's for
tomorrow. I've had enough driving for one day.'

'You mean we're actually going to stop?' It might have
been heavy-handed but for once Kuldip's sarcasm was entirely good-humoured. 'We're going to eat and drink and
pretend we're civilized human beings?'

'Travel with me,' I said, 'and you travel in style. As
soon as we're past the Pont du Gard you can start looking
out for a hotel. We might as well eat where we sleep.'

'Thank Christ.' Kuldip's relief was genuine. 'I half expected we'd be sleeping in the car or camping. Will we be
safe in a hotel?'

'It should be safe enough now we're this side of the Rhône but you'd better make the most of it. After tonight we shall be camping.'

Kuldip groaned and I carried on driving. The hotel was a risk I had to take because I needed to contact Pawson. The odds were against him being immediately available and if we had to wait, a hotel was as good a place to do it as any. Although Kuldip didn't know about the phone call, she did have another question. It took her almost five minutes to admit to her ignorance.

'What is the Pont du Gard?' she asked. 'I don't know what I'm looking for.'

'It's an antique sewer,' I told her.

'A sewer?'

'That's right. There's been a hell of a lot of erosion since the Romans built it.'

She managed her second laugh of the day when we reached the aqueduct. However, I very much doubted whether her mirth had a great deal to do with overhead Roman sewers. It was more likely the result of euphoria at the prospect of sleeping between crisp, clean sheets and stuffing herself with food which hadn't been ruined by her cooking.

The hotel Kuldip would have liked was the Terminus in Uzes but I overruled her, settling for a humbler hostelry on the outskirts of town. As I pointed out to her, we were only pretending to be tourists. We weren't actually going to count the deathwatch beetles in St Theodorat or stroll hand in hand along the Promenade des Marroniers, admiring the beauties of the Vallee d'Alzon below. We were going to stay closeted in our hotel room until it was time to leave the following morning.

My choice was a small, family-run establishment, one of the *relais de silence*, and we struck lucky. Nobody batted an eyelid at the Afro-British racial mix and the proprietor's wife was all bustling hospitality, determined that our overnight stay should be a comfortable one. Of course we could eat dinner in our room. It would be no problem at all to call us at five the following morning. Would we like breakfast brought up before we left? It all made me wonder how British hotels ever managed to do any business.

Kuldip seemed perfectly content to leave all the arrangements to me. She didn't even raise an eyebrow at the four-posted double bed which was the most striking feature of our room. However, once the proprietress had gone, she couldn't resist a sly dig.

'Where are you going to sleep, Philis?' she asked, arranging herself decoratively on the counterpane and making sure I could see plenty of boob and thigh.

'In the bed,' I told her. 'I'm older and I'm doing the driving so I have first choice. You can snuggle down where you like.'

Although I'd tentatively included a seduction scene in my programme for the evening, other considerations had come first. The double bed meant there wasn't going to be any idle speculation about the exact nature of our relationship. It also meant that Kuldip would be near to hand if there should be any trouble.

After I'd polished off my *sauté de veau marengo* and the lion's share of a bottle of the local wine, it was time for my phone call. Kuldip yawned her way through my repeated instructions about not leaving the room, then I headed downstairs. The number I dialled was in Paris. Fouche was the local Control and I hoped he'd be useful to me.

His brief off-the-cuff rundown on Louis Martel pretty well matched my own impressions and more than justified my request for Fouche to contact London on my behalf. Despite his objections, I made it perfectly plain that the Duty Officer was no good for me; I wanted Pawson and nobody else. I was being unreasonable, and I knew it, but

I'd have hated to act out of character.

It took almost three quarters of an hour to drag Pawson away from whatever he was doing and I spent the time happily enough with a couple of Pernods. Although my temporary sense of security was too dangerous an attitude to foster, this was the first opportunity I'd had to relax over the past couple of days.

When his call came through, Pawson made his annoyance clear. He didn't like being interrupted and he didn't like having to talk to me on the telephone. He preferred his messages to arrive written down and in code. However, he became more reasonable once I'd explained my dilemma.

'It sounds awkward,' he conceded. 'Are you sure you can't handle this Martel on your own?'

'Not without my Superman cape, I can't. I assume you still want me to play this straight, carry on as the loyal mercenary?'

'I don't see any reason to change our plans at this stage.'

I'd probably have agreed with him if I'd been sitting safely in London.

'And you don't have any fresh information to give me?'

'You already know everything I have, Philis.'

Pawson's answer came out pat. It should have done, because he'd used some variation of the same lie in just about every conversation I could remember. Pawson seemed to think I was some kind of composite character from *Mission Impossible* and *Voyage into the Unknown*.

'In that case, I'd say Martel is in a position to prejudice the entire mission. If he keeps on snapping at my heels, I'll have to keep on discouraging him. Sooner or later the police are likely to notice the trail of dead bodies.'

'But you are temporarily in the clear?'

' "Temporarily" is the key word. I think somebody ought to have a discreet word in Martel's shell-like ear.

Promote a hands-off-Philis campaign. He doesn't play any part in your devious plans and he's a nuisance I can certainly do without.'

Pawson came up with all the usual claptrap about infringement of territorial rights before he finally agreed. I took his objections with about half a ton of salt. As I pointed out to him, if French suzerainty was so dear to his heart, I'd be only too glad to hand in my forged documents at the nearest *gendarmerie*. All the same, our conversation had left me in a much happier frame of mind. Now I simply had to stay ahead of Martel until the message had been delivered.

Sex itself is simple. That's why birds, bees and three-toed sloths can do it. It's the emotions which go with the sex that are so complicated. Sexually, Kuldip and I were pretty good together, far better than I'd expected. A bit of kissing and cuddling and teasing and there we both were, primed and ready for a spot of international relations. On a basic level it was a coupling most of the sex manuals would have been happy to endorse. We'd both have scored well for technical merit and artistic impression. The orgasm count was high. It was the aftertaste which was all wrong. There were so many ulterior motives floating around, it was little more than a physical exercise.

Kuldip had spelled her motives out clearly enough back at the chalet and mine were no more commendable. I had some questions to ask and our post-coital embrace was going to lose Kuldip a lot of her room for manoeuvre.

'Not bad, lover,' she murmured. 'Not bad at all. Keep on practising and you'll really hit the button one of these days.'

'You'd better write me a reference. I'm always looking for a new position.'

It was one of those moments when I promised to find

myself a new scriptwriter but Kuldip didn't seem to mind. She laughed so deep in her throat it was almost a growl and moved in closer. A one-off session was no good to her. She was after addiction.

'There's something I've been meaning to ask you,' I said.

I wasn't as good at sexy murmurs as Kuldip but I did my best.

'Ask away, then. This isn't a time for secrets.'

'It's about the rubies.'

This time Kuldip was the one to stiffen. She would have pulled away from me if she could.

'Rubies?' she said. 'I don't have any rubies.'

It was a lengthy process and an inconclusive one. There were lies and half-truths and evasions. There were even a couple of sexual intermissions which neither of us really wanted but which our respective roles made obligatory. At the end of it all, Kuldip thought she'd won and I knew I hadn't. Although she'd told me far more than she thought she had, there was a limit to how far I could go on deduction and surmise. And to how long I could stand the pace with a nubile young Ugandan. This was why I called it a night while I was still slightly ahead on points.

The morning found us following a favourite tourist route, driving north from Ales towards Le Puy on the N106. The road twisted and wound its way through mountains and forests. It ran beside the spectacular Gorges de Chassezac. There were rocky cliffs, rushing streams and ruddy great hunks of granite. It was all most scenic but this wasn't why we were there. My motives were far more prosaic.

Le Puy itself didn't figure in my plans. It was a tourist centre and in France, in common with everywhere else in the world, there were links between tourism and organized crime. There would be more than enough easy pickings in Le Puy to attract a small shark or two and these small sharks were the very people Martel would have contacted. By now he'd have guessed that we hadn't tried for Switzerland or Italy and he would have cast his net wider. We might already have passed beyond its reach but this wasn't something I was prepared to bet on.

Provided he knew what he was doing, it wouldn't take him very long to discover we'd spent the night at Uzes. It was simply a matter of having enough men and enough telephones. This made it worth my while to plant a little calculated misinformation. Kuldip was driving up front with me and she was noticed at both of the two stops we made. We bought a few litres of petrol in Le Grand Colomb and took early morning coffee at La Bastide-Puylaurent. Both the garage and the cafe would be obvious places to check, situated right beside the road, and, if Martel was still on our heels, they should confirm the pattern I was trying to establish. We were heading north, just like we should have been doing.

Ideally, I'd have liked to change vehicles when I changed direction but this was something which had to wait. The best I could manage was to relegate Kuldip to the floor in the back before I turned left off the N106 at Langogne. I thought this ought to be good enough but I was mistaken. I'd failed to allow for Martel's luck and Kuldip's bloody-mindedness.

MILLAU, FRANCE

Martel had made it sound as though he was bestowing some signal honour, but to Jacques Doriot the trip was nothing more than a monumental pain in the backside. He didn't like the countryside and he didn't like making polite conversation to crazy old women, especially to a

crazy old woman who made a grab for his balls every time
the nurse turned her head. If Martel was so fond of his
damn sister, why did he hide her away in the mountains
and avoid her like the plague? And if he had to send her
flowers and chocolates on her birthday, why the hell
couldn't they go through the post?

This was the third consecutive year Doriot had been
forced to make the pilgrimage and he'd set off early,
hoping to make the round trip to Marseilles in the day.
Then his petrol pump had packed up outside Lodeve and
that had been the end of that. It had been late afternoon
by the time he'd eventually reached the sanatorium and
there'd been no question of simply dumping the presents
with one of the nurses. Martel would want to know how
dear Amelie was. He'd expect to hear what she was wearing and what she'd said. Not that Doriot would be able to
tell the truth, in any case. He could hardly tell Martel
that his sister looked as though she'd been disinterred
from the local graveyard, was modelling the same food-
stained dress as the previous year and, in between groping
him, didn't do much except cackle and dribble.

Fortunately, the day had taken a turn for the better
after he'd bumped into the young American. By the time
he left, it had been too late to consider driving back to
Marseilles, and Millau was the nearest town of any size to
the sanatorium. Doriot had driven down into the town
centre and booked himself into a hotel on the Place du
Mandarous. All he'd wanted was a meal and to snatch a
few hours' sleep before the drive back, but even this
hadn't worked out. Doriot was too late for the evening
meal at the hotel, a discovery which had done nothing to
improve his temper. All the same, this had proved to be a
blessing in disguise because it had been outside La Musar-
dière that he'd been picked up by Alison.

She was a type Doriot had had no difficulty in recog-
nizing, a young American student spending the summer

bumming around Europe. She didn't speak much French and Doriot's English was by no means perfect but the situation was clear enough. She was hungry, she'd temporarily run out of money and she didn't normally do this sort of thing but, under the circumstances, she didn't have any choice. Back in Marseilles Doriot probably wouldn't have spared her a second glance. However, after the sanatorium, he'd liked the idea of eating with someone who was young and sane and feminine.

Even when they'd eaten, Doriot hadn't been absolutely sure whether or not he was going to take her back to the hotel. She'd been too hungry to bother much with conversation and what little she had said had been mostly incomprehensible. At least, Doriot was sure he must have misunderstood her because he couldn't believe that any student at any college in the world could major in oral hygiene. It wasn't until they were in his hotel room that he'd discovered Alison had the same approach to the subject as Linda Lovelace. She spent so much time down there that Doriot began to wonder what effect her digestive juices might have on him.

Among other things, she'd blown any chances Doriot might have had of an early start the next day and it was early afternoon before he finally pulled back the curtains. What he saw in the café across the square woke him up far more effectively than any cold shower would have done. Suddenly he knew it hadn't been a wasted journey after all.

CHAPTER 12

Millau was supposed to be the final break in the trail, one last obstacle for anybody who traced us this far. Although it would only delay pursuit for a few hours, hours had

become the name of the game since my phone call to
Pawson and it was a precaution I couldn't afford to overlook. The red Datsun was a trademark we could do without and it was time to change our image. I dumped
Kuldip at a café in the centre of town, with strict instructions to find a table well away from the windows, then
drove off to locate a used car dealer.

The one I selected operated on the Avenue de Verdun,
out by the municipal stadium. He looked like a crook,
spawned from whole generations of crooks, and he was
the only man I'd ever met who used Brylcreem on a totally
hairless head. He had other little idiosyncrasies as well,
including the business ethics of a starving barracuda,
which made him precisely what I wanted. It worked both
ways because I was the kind of customer he must have had
wet dreams about. Almost from the moment I first opened
my mouth, he was convinced the Datsun must figure on a
police hot sheet somewhere or other, an impression I did
nothing to correct. The red tape involved in the trans-
action dissolved as if by magic and each short cut earned
him a few more francs.

I swapped a virtually brand new Datsun for a four-
year-old Peugeot 304 with its bodywork shot to pieces and
the dealer could hardly believe his luck. When he invited
me to drop in again whenever I was passing, he was
speaking with total sincerity. A dozen customers like me
each year and he'd be well on the way to a wealthy retirement.

Although I was perfectly satisfied with the deal myself,
I wasn't feeling nearly so pleased a few minutes later.
Kuldip had deliberately disregarded my instructions and
was sitting outside the café, in plain view at one of the
tables on the pavement. She'd been in a funny mood ever
since I'd relegated her to the floor of the Datsun again
and the sheer stupidity of her little gesture annoyed me
intensely. There was a streak of pettiness in her which was

potentially dangerous.

Just how dangerous only became apparent after I'd parked the Peugeot. The checks I made as I strolled back into the Place du Mandarous were purely automatic. We hadn't been followed to Millau and Kuldip hadn't had long enough to make herself really conspicuous but a large part of my training had been to cultivate good habits. You didn't just stroll up to somebody you were meeting and say hello. You always checked the area, even when you thought you were safe. This was what I did now, going the long way round the square instead of cutting directly across to where Kuldip was sitting.

Even so I nearly missed him. He blended into the scenery quite well, absorbed in his newspaper and displaying no apparent interest in the café opposite. Perhaps he was a little bit too self-consciously casual or perhaps his suit smacked a little too much of the city rather than a small provincial town. Whatever it was, I noticed him and he interested me sufficiently to make me stop for a spot of window shopping.

After a couple of minutes I was positive that my instincts were right, not simply the symptoms of paranoia. He was definitely watching Kuldip and I started looking around for the rest of his team, uneasily aware that my description would have been circulated together with Kuldip's. I was even more uneasy when I failed to spot anybody else because this didn't make sense. By now there were so many variables that any decision I reached would almost inevitably be wrong and I returned my attention to the man with the newspaper. Smart suit, medium build, long, dark hair, unshaven, in his mid-thirties. He still looked wrong and the temptation to take him out was very strong. It was a temptation which died away when he was joined by three other men.

The newcomers looked like locals and there was nothing at all casual about them. The man with the newspaper said a few words, then three heads swivelled to look across to where Kuldip was sunning herself. Any last, lingering doubts I might have had were dispelled. It was time to run again and when we did I suspected that we might regret my clever horse-trading with the Datsun.

The opposition seemed to breed faster than rabbits. While I was smoking a cigarette, three other men approached the man with the copy of *Ici Paris*, two of them together and one on his own. This was more than enough to block all the exits from the square. With two men actually in the café, a couple of tables away from Kuldip, three others loitering inconspicuously in the vicinity and a sixth man sitting at the wheel of a Citroën Diane parked in one of the streets leading into the square, the area was pretty well covered. My friend with the newspaper must have thought so too. After a last look around, he tossed the newspaper into a rubbish bin and turned to go into the hotel behind him.

I gave him a minute, then followed him inside. The lobby was deserted so I approached the rather austere lady at reception.

'My friend,' I said, using the kind of French which made Ted Heath sound like a linguist. 'He just came in.'

'You mean Monsieur Doriot?'

I nodded vigorously. This was one of the great advantages of a lousy accent. People had to work so hard at understanding what I said, they didn't have a chance to be suspicious. 'Do you know where he went?'

'I think he's making a phone call.' The receptionist waved a hand in the general direction of the staircase. I thanked her gallantly, then wandered off in the direction she'd indicated. The telephone booth was squeezed in under the stairs and I leaned against a section of wall where I was hidden both from Doriot and the reception desk. The drawback was that I could only hear Doriot's end of the conversation.

'Flaubert came across without any bother,' he was saying. 'His men are with me now.'

Silence.

'No, only the woman. There's been no sign of the Englishman.'

A briefer silence, broken by Doriot's laugh.

'Don't worry. There's no way they'll slip through the net this time.'

For the next two or three minutes Doriot only contributed the odd grunt. Despite his assurances, somebody obviously was worried and intended to make sure his instructions were clearly understood.

'OK,' Doriot said. 'I'll be expecting them later this afternoon.'

Another brief crackle from the other end of the line.

'I understand. I only move in if it's absolutely necessary. Otherwise I wait for reinforcements.'

This concluded their conversation and while they were swopping 'au revoirs' I edged a bit further along the wall. Apart from Doriot and the receptionist, the hotel seemed to be deserted and the temptation to take Doriot out had resurfaced. If he was in command, it wouldn't do any harm to have him safely out of the way for the next half an hour or so.

He wasn't any trouble at all. I hit him a couple of times as he stepped out of the booth and that was that. Doriot was even thoughtful enough to fall forwards into my arms so he didn't make a nasty clatter on the floor. He probably didn't want to disturb the other occupants of the hotel any more than I did.

There was just the one inviolable rule in my line of work. I was at perfect liberty to break all the Commandments in the Bible, plus one or two God had overlooked, but one thing was categorically forbidden. 'Thou shalt not bugger up or in any way inconvenience tax-paying citizens' was the way it went and it applied whether the aforementioned citizens were in London, Leningrad or Lusaka. It was their money which kept the wheels of espionage turning and on no account must they be upset.

As rules went, this wasn't a bad one. I might even have given it my one hundred per cent support if I'd been sitting behind a desk in Whitehall. As a field operative, however, my priorities were slightly different. If causing a little inconvenience was going to keep the Philis hide intact, then hard luck, citizenry.

There were half a dozen vehicles in the park at the rear of the hotel. I selected the brown Simca purely on the basis that the doors were unlocked and the keys in the ignition. The first thing I did once I was out of the car park was to stuff the documentation I'd taken from Doriot into the glove compartment. It was no use to me and I didn't mind giving the local gendarmes a clue or two.

When I drove into the square, I made no attempt to be furtive. On the contrary, I went out of my way to toot the horn a couple of times before I parked illegally in front of the café. I wanted to be associated with the Simca. Otherwise my little exercise in larceny would have been a complete waste of time.

'You really are a stupid bitch,' I said, flashing Kuldip a big smile as I sat down beside her.

'What is it? Is something the matter?'

'How could it be? After all, you've kept out of sight like I told you.'

'We're in trouble?'

'We are and we'll be in more if you start looking around. A nice, carefree smile would be a much better idea.'

She did her best, although she didn't look particularly convincing.

'I'm sorry,' she said. 'What do we do?'

'We try to behave as if we don't have a care in the
world. I'll settle the bill and then we can do some window-
shopping.'

I gave her all the details on the outward leg of our
leisurely stroll. By the time we were heading back towards
the Place du Mandarous she knew exactly what to do. It
helped that only two of Doriot's men had bothered to
follow us. The rest were still covering the Simca. While it
stayed in front of the café they didn't have any fear of
losing us.

Before I'd left the hotel I'd committed one other minor
piece of larceny. The chef and the rest of the kitchen staff
had been most understanding when I'd wandered in on
them and they'd been quite happy to accept my profuse
apologies. If any of them had noticed the carrot I'd palmed
on my way out, they'd simply put it down as another example of British eccentricity. Either that or they'd place
me as a close relative of Bugs Bunny.

'It's the green Citroën,' I said. 'Make it look good.'

'I will.'

Kuldip's performance might not have fooled a professional for a second but it was more than adequate for the
clowns we had to cope with. She carted all the usual
female bric-à-brac around with her and when her hand-
bag hit the pavement, the contents went everywhere. In a
few seconds we were down on our hands and knees, along
with two or three helpful passers-by, and there was all the
confusion I needed. Kuldip probably lost some of her in-
timate odds and ends but, more important, I'd lost one
large carrot and the driver of the Citroën had gained one.
With any luck, it was going to wreck his exhaust system
when he started up.

By my reckoning we still had several minutes to play
with before Doriot became a factor again and I used one
of them to reinforce my association with the Simca. As
there weren't any policemen in sight, it was well worth

spending a few seconds playing with the handle of the
driver's door while Kuldip persuaded me to take a walk
towards the shops on the far side of the square. It was all
good, psychological stuff but Kuldip didn't appreciate
the subtleties of what I was doing.

'Come on, Philis,' she hissed. 'Let's get out of here
while we can.'

Although we weren't quite so leisurely as before, the
pattern was pretty much the same. Kuldip found a couple
of things to point out in the windows and I feigned the
polite indifference which seemed appropriate. The same
two men were following and, now they were sure of us,
they were allowing us a bit more room. It still wasn't quite
enough. The doors of the Peugeot were locked and the
car dealer hadn't given any guarantees about the engine
firing first time.

'It's the next corner,' I told Kuldip. 'We're going into
the tobacconist's. Just follow my lead and we'll be fine.'

I didn't head directly for the shop. We'd actually gone
past and were at the kerb of the side street when I began
my impersonation of a nicotine addict without the
makings for a fix. This meant we had to turn to face the
way we'd come and our two shadows immediately became
absorbed in the contents of a toyshop window.

'We walk briskly,' I said as I pushed open the door of
the tobacconist's. 'We don't run.'

The owner of the shop wasn't noticeably enthusiastic
about the way we entered through one door and walked
straight out of the other, the one which led into the side
street, but we weren't on the premises long enough for
him to vent his indignation. It was only fifty yards to the
Peugeot, and we reached it before either of Doriot's men
had rounded the corner. They still weren't in sight when
the engine caught but they did see us when we emerged
from the side street because I'd parked the Peugeot facing
the wrong way. Although they were no more than a dozen

paces away, they were taken completely by surprise and I'd found a gap in the traffic before they'd decided what to do.

By the time we reached the square, they were way behind, making the best speed they could along the busy pavement, and none of the other watchers noticed us go by. They were far too busy keeping an eye on the Simca. Kuldip did spend a few minutes twisted round in her seat but there was nothing for her to see. For the moment, at least, we were free and clear.

'Is that all there is to it?' she asked, her voice tinged with disbelief.

'Some of us just have the knack,' I said modestly.

Unfortunately, I wasn't fooling myself. All I'd done was buy myself and Kuldip a breathing space.

MARSEILLES, FRANCE

'Bloody Philis,' Carrodus said, tossing his cigarette end out of the window. 'The man's a menace.'

'This isn't exactly his fault.'

'It never is.' Carrodus refused to be mollified. He'd been in a foul temper ever since Pawson had contacted him in Barcelona. 'Philis has the opposite of whatever it was King Midas had. Everything he touches turns to instant shit. Nobody else but Philis could manage to bring the entire *Unione Corse* on his back within his first few hours in France.'

'It's not the *Unione*. Martel isn't a Corsican.'

'I don't really care what the hell he is. The principle is still the same. Philis attracts trouble the way dogs attract fleas.'

For a few seconds Dixon concentrated on his driving. Although he was very much the junior of the two men, and acutely aware of the fact, he wasn't taking his companion's grumbling particularly seriously.

'I thought you two were supposed to be friends,' he said.

'We are,' Carrodus agreed. 'At least, we were. After this little fiasco I'm not so sure. You've no idea what I had to leave behind in Barcelona.'

'She was nice, was she?'

Carrodus had a well-substantiated reputation as one of the department's top swordsmen. If half the stories he'd heard about him were true, Dixon reckoned he'd end up in the National Stud after Pawson had finished with him.

'Nice isn't the word for her,' Carrodus answered. 'And she isn't the type to wait.'

'Never mind. There are plenty more fish in the sea. I've seen one or two quite tasty morsels here in Marseilles.'

A contemptuous snort was the only reply Dixon received. Carla had been something special. To Carrodus's way of thinking, planting smoke bombs in half the nightclubs in Marseilles was no substitute for what she'd had to offer.

CHAPTER 13

We'd driven through part of the Causses on our way to Millau. Now we were going up into them. According to the guidebooks, the area was a limestone plateau about three to four thousand feet high and covering about 1500 square miles. This wasn't a description which did the region justice. Or perhaps 'justice' wasn't quite the right word. Because of limestone's peculiar properties, the plateau was a rocky semi-desert, virtually devoid of surface water or worthwhile vegetation. Instead there were boulders, gorges, potholes and caves. Away from the canyons and valleys, cut down through the limestone by rivers like the Tarn and Aveyron, there was no resident population apart from the sheep and the odd tourist.

Losing ourselves was easy. I progressed from main roads to minor roads to barely identifiable roads to tracks. When the tracks threatened to run out, I turned into a likely-looking dry valley and stopped. For the last five minutes of our drive I hadn't seen a single other living thing.

'Here we are, then,' I said, opening the driver's door.

'Where?' Kuldip enquired. 'I don't remember seeing any signposts.'

'It's somewhere we're not likely to be found.' This sounded far better than admitting I'd be unable to pin-point our position on the map. 'Hunt around in the boot and you should find something we can eat.'

She'd find quite a lot more besides, because I'd stocked up in Millau immediately after I'd acquired the Peugeot. The quantity must have impressed Kuldip because she had another question ready when she returned with the bread, the cheese and a bottle of *vin* very *ordinaire*.

'How long did you say we're staying here?' she demanded. 'A couple of days? There's enough stuff in the boot to last us a week.'

'We stop as long as necessary. I'll try a phone call tomorrow to find out what the situation is. If everything is OK, we'll go. If not, we'll have to stay another day.'

I'd already told Kuldip about the telephone call. As far as she was concerned, it was Sir Keith I'd be contacting. Although she was all in favour of having Martel called off, camping out wasn't her cup of tea. Her next question made her distaste apparent.

'Where exactly are we sleeping?'

I shrugged.

'There are plenty of caves to choose from. Once I have a fire alight, it should be quite cosy.'

'Whoopee,' Kuldip said. 'I can hardly wait.'

Kuldip's evident dislike for the great outdoors didn't bother me a bit. The important thing was that Martel could send a small army up into the Causses and still not have much hope of finding us. My cautious optimism lasted all the while I was picking a cave, lighting a fire and bedding down for the night. I'd have been wiser to stick by my earlier pessimism. When an operation had turned sour, any changes were usually for the worse.

The first I knew of the helicopter was at breakfast-time. I'd rekindled the fire and was brewing up some coffee when I heard the faint buzz in the distance. A couple of seconds later Kuldip had heard it too.

'What is that noise?' she asked.

'It's a bloody helicopter. You'd better stand by to put out the fire.'

We'd camped about twenty-five yards into the cave, round a slight dogleg so the fire wouldn't be visible from outside. When I reached the entrance, one glance was sufficient to dash any hopes I'd had of this being a random flight. The chopper was heading straight towards the cliff where our cave was, as though it was homing in on a beacon. It had one of sorts, too. Search parties on foot could have come within a few yards of the Peugeot without realizing it was there. From the air, with the early morning sun glinting off the roof, it must have been visible from miles away. It seemed I'd underestimated Martel once again.

My sole consolation was that we were safe enough in the cave for the time being. I was standing well back in the shadows and the helicopter was still too far away to notice the few wisps of smoke drifting from the entrance. I waited a few seconds longer, just to make sure there weren't any military markings on the aircraft, then I called back to Kuldip to put out the fire.

A minute later we weren't at all safe in the cave. The few wisps had become a great billowing cloud of smoke nobody could possibly miss. I coughed my way back to where she was standing, cursing her stupidity now instead of my own.

'Did you have to pour the coffee on the fire?' I demanded angrily. 'We're not trying to send smoke signals.'

'What else was I supposed to do?'

Although Kuldip sounded defensive, I knew I was being unfair and frustration was no adequate excuse. My sloppiness was the reason we were trapped in the cave, and trying to shift the blame wasn't going to do either of us any good.

'You'd better gather our things together,' I said in a more reasonable tone. 'We're going to have to move.'

'The men in the helicopter are definitely looking for us?'

'They were,' I told her. 'Now they've found us. I'm going back to the entrance to see what happens. Give me a shout when you're ready.'

What was happening was that the helicopter was now hovering above the Peugeot and this meant we wouldn't be able to move anywhere. I needed the FN rifle I'd left at the chalet because the shotgun I had just didn't have the range to be of any use. I couldn't even derive any encouragement from the fact that there were only two men aboard the chopper. There would also be a radio and it wouldn't be long before reinforcements were on their way.

'I'm ready,' Kuldip called.

'Fine. Leave the things where they are and come up here with me.'

She only had to watch the hovering whirlybird for a few seconds before she reached the same conclusion as me.

'Am I wrong,' she said, 'or are they pinning us down?'

'I only wish you were wrong. The passenger has a rifle.

He's got our cave spotted and he's waiting for something
to shoot at.'

'Aren't they going to come in after us?'

'Not if they have any sense. They're stopping us from
going anywhere and they should have help on the way.
They'll wait until then before they move in.'

'Oh.'

Kuldip's voice suddenly sounded very small. However
pessimistic I might be myself, her morale needed a boost.

'There's one hell of a difference between finding us and
having us in the bag,' I said. 'I'm going to leave you here
with the shotgun while I have a look around at the back of
the cave. You can give me a shout if anything exciting
happens.'

Despite my half-hearted attempt at reassurance,
Kuldip still looked rather forlorn when I left her and I
could understand how she felt. The daily crisis seemed to
have become a regular feature of our lives.

The previous afternoon, I hadn't simply marched into the
first cave we'd come to. In fact, I'd rejected at least half a
dozen before I'd made my choice. Our cave was really a
tunnel, leading back into the hillside, and I'd found what
I wanted about a hundred yards in, a narrow chimney in
the ceiling which led up to the surface. It wasn't much of
a chimney but it was definitely climbable and this was all
that had interested me at the time. Now, being climbable
was no longer enough. I needed to know exactly where
the chimney would take us.

It proved to be a fairly easy climb, although there were
a few rocky projections which dug painfully into my flesh.
With my shoulder blades pressed against one side of the
chimney, there was plenty of leverage for my feet on the
other, and Kuldip was tall enough not to have any bother
either. However, as an alternative exit it had plenty of
drawbacks. For a start, the hillside above was virtually

devoid of cover. There were one or two clusters of rocks dotted around but none of them was close enough to be particularly attractive. We'd be spotted from the helicopter the moment we emerged and although we'd be near the limit of effective rifle range, once it moved closer we'd be sitting ducks.

I rested at the top of the chimney for a few seconds, with only the top of my head above the level of the ground. Then I climbed back down again, losing a bit more skin before I was in the tunnel.

'Everything OK?' I shouted.

'They're still in the same place.' The bends in the tunnel made her voice faint. 'What are you doing back there?'

'Potholing. I'll be with you in a few minutes.'

The tunnel stretched quite a way further back into the hillside and the further it went, the lower the ceiling. I kept going until I was down on my hands and knees, hoping the ceiling would rise again, but it didn't, and I decided to call it a day. The tunnel was still negotiable but I didn't have a torch and I thought I could hear running water ahead. On balance, I preferred to take my chances back at the entrance.

The situation there was pretty much the same as when I'd last checked with the helicopter still hovering above the Peugeot.

'Well?' Kuldip enquired.

'We wait,' I told her. 'The chimney leads up to one of the barest hillsides in the south of France.'

'So we're trapped.'

'It's not quite as bad as that.' It was, but I wasn't about to admit it. 'The helicopter will have to refuel sooner or later. When it leaves we should have a bit more scope.'

While we were waiting, I kept Kuldip busy. There was plenty of loose rock lying around and if it did come to a last stand, we'd need some kind of barricade. Leaving the cave might be beyond us but we could make it bloody difficult for anybody else to come in.

The three cars arrived in convoy, throwing up a cloud of dust we could see long before we could distinguish the actual vehicles. All told they contained eleven men and they all appeared to know what they were doing. One of them, who looked suspiciously like my friend Doriot, risked having his hair blown off by the rotors and conducted a brief conversation with the men in the helicopter. I hoped it might land and give us a chance at the chimney but we were out of luck. As soon as the brief exchange was concluded, the helicopter regained height and Doriot started issuing instructions.

He proved to be depressingly thorough. One car and two men drove back the way they'd come, presumably to warn off any hitchhikers or shepherds who wandered into the war zone. This left Doriot another eight men to play with and seven of them fanned out among the rocks in the valley below. However, it was the eighth man I was interested in. He was the only one of the newcomers with a rifle and he was sent to the far side of the valley, to the hillside opposite our cave. It meant we could forget about the chimney, whether the helicopter stayed or not. We were bottled up, and no matter how determined we made our last-ditch stand inside the cave, we'd only be delaying the inevitable.

Doriot appreciated the situation as well as I did. Once the rifleman was in position, he waved his hand and the helicopter was away. No doubt it would return after it had refuelled.

One of the pieces of equipment Doriot had thought to bring with him was a loud-hailer. He carried it with him into the valley below, making no effort to hide, and he stopped while he was a good hundred yards away.

'Hello, there,' he shouted.

His English seemed to be on a par with my French but, despite the slight distortion caused by the megaphone, I had no difficulty understanding him.

'Hello there,' he tried again. 'You in the cave. Can you hear me?'

I'd no intention of answering him. It was going to cost him to make sure we were really where he thought we were.

'We know you're there,' Doriot persevered. 'Why not be sensible and save everybody a lot of trouble. You're outnumbered and you're surrounded so you can't possibly get away. Do yourselves a favour and give up now.'

I still wasn't answering and Doriot went to confer with one of the men hidden among the rocks. It only took him a minute to decide on a slight variation in tactics.

'Come on, Philis.' His use of my name was the final proof of his link with Martel. 'You know you can't win. Send the woman out on her own and we'll call it quits. Once we have her you're free to go anywhere you want. You have my word on it.'

He paused to see whether I'd answer and I used the time to glance across at Kuldip. She was looking as worried as I'd thought she'd be. I'd been offered my life in exchange for her and she was wondering how tempted I was. If our roles had been reversed, I'd already have been outside the cave.

'It's your only chance, Philis.' The loudhailer was back in operation again. 'You have five minutes to think it over, then I'll have to come up there after you. If it comes to that, you're a dead man.'

Doriot had finished and I looked across at Kuldip again.

'Well?' I said.

'Well what?'

She was even more worried now.

'Do you want to surrender?'

'No way.' As she spoke, Kuldip was shaking her head with some vigour. 'Whatever that man promises, he intends to kill both of us sooner or later.'

'I couldn't agree more. Unfortunately, there doesn't seem to be a great deal we can do about it.'

'We can fight them off. I know how to use a gun.'

'Maybe you can but we can't hold out indefinitely. Even if we managed to last until tonight, we wouldn't stand a chance once it was dark.'

'Perhaps I ought to surrender after all.'

Morale was sagging again so I tried to give it a boost. As I pointed out to Kuldip, escape wasn't the name of the game. What we were playing for was time, because sooner or later a message should be coming through from Martel, calling the hunt off.

'Are you sure of that?' Kuldip sounded dubious. 'I don't see how Sir Keith can manage it.'

'Nor do I, but he said he could, and I believed him. He's not given to making rash promises. Besides, from what I can gather he has too much at stake to take any risks. He said it wouldn't take more than forty-eight hours to arrange. What we have to do is give him the time he needs.'

Fortunately, Kuldip was more interested in the mechanics of how I intended to manage this than in asking any more awkward questions. The first step in my plan of campaign was simplicity itself. We merely defended the cave entrance for as long as humanly possible. It was the next bit which was the problem.

Unless I was overlooking something, there were only two options. Either we went potholing and followed the tunnel back into the hillside or we practised a bit of deception and tried to convince Doriot that this was what we'd done. Personally, I was dead against the first suggestion. Potholing was almost as dangerous as being shot at, even if you had maps, experience and equipment.

The alternative was only a temporary answer but, if it worked, the deception would gain us time without exposing us to any new risks. I'd nearly missed the crevice in the tunnel wall and I'd been actively searching for something like it. With any luck, Doriot and company would never even realize it was there.

'Go back and take a look at it,' I suggested. 'Then you'll have a better idea of what I'm talking about.'

When she'd gone, I went back to watching the rocks below. It wouldn't be long before Doriot made his first move.

There was only one way for Doriot to discover whether we were in the cave and two men volunteered for the initial survey. Or, more likely, they were press-ganged into it. Their approach had to be frontal and they took maximum advantage of the available cover, one to the right and the other to the left as they leapfrogged each other. They also took their time. They knew enough about what they were doing to realize what could easily happen to them.

Kuldip returned while they were still way down the slope and I signalled to her to keep well down. The entrance to the cave was in deep shadow and there was no point in revealing our position until it became absolutely necessary. Even our barricade wouldn't be visible from below.

'Well?' I whispered. 'What do you think?'

'It's a bit small.'

Kuldip clearly didn't want to overwhelm me with her enthusiasm.

'It's a tight squeeze but we can manage it. Anyway, it's your choice. What's it to be, the crevice or the labyrinth?'

After she'd given me the answer I'd been angling for, I sent Kuldip back along the tunnel. I also warned her not to panic when the shooting started. Whoever got shot, it certainly wasn't going to be me.

I had another ten minutes to wait. By then the recon-
naissance party was within twenty-five yards of the cave
and had run out of cover. The last stretch was exposed
and uphill and all three of us knew what came next. The
man to the right had the M3 with the silencer built into
the barrel, so he'd be blasting away at the cave while his
companion made the suicide run.

What they'd failed to allow for was the way I used a
shotgun. When the shooting started, I didn't even consider sticking my head up into the hail of .45 calibre
bullets. There wasn't much point as I knew where the real
attack was coming from. I could watch the man to the left
through a gap in my barricade and I allowed him to get
halfway to the cave before I poked the shotgun over the
top of the barricade, pointed it in his general direction
and squeezed the trigger. I left the shotgun where it was
long enough for a second shot at his friend with the submachine gun, then all of me was down below the barricade again.

I wasn't a moment too soon because the sniper on the
hillside opposite was far better than I'd expected. He only
had my muzzle flash to aim at but he fired four times
and, when he'd finished, one entire section of my limestone barricade had disintegrated. This was all the
encouragement I needed to scuttle along the ground until
I reached the point where the remnants of the barricade
met the left-hand wall.

Only then did I risk a quick peep through a gap in the
limestone rocks. The man I'd killed was lying with his
head downhill, so about all I could see of him were the
soles of his feet. Of his friend with the M3 there wasn't a
sign. I assumed he was cowering behind his rock, awaiting further instructions. I also assumed he was unharmed
because it would have taken a miracle for me to have nailed
him as well.

This didn't really matter but the bastard with the rifle

did, and there was nothing I could do about him. At that kind of range the shotgun was worse than useless and my Colt Python wouldn't be a great deal better. The last time I'd tested it, I'd scored 95 per cent on a silhouette target at fifty metres. The sniper was more than double this distance away, there was a cross-breeze and I'd only have the top of his head to aim at. Given two hundred rounds and a hell of a lot of luck I might put one bullet close enough to worry him but I'd have been dead approximately one hundred and ninety-eight shots previously.

For the moment, though, the honours were even. Doriot now knew he was laying siege to the right cave and I'd shown that he'd have to work at getting in there with us. During the next half-hour, nothing much happened. Kuldip did make a brief appearance to check if I was OK but I sent her back with a flea in her ear and returned to watching the lack of activity down below. It seemed we were all waiting for the helicopter to reappear. As soon as it became audible in the distance, Doriot emerged from hiding and headed towards where the vehicles were parked.

This time the chopper landed briefly before flying off again. Although nobody disembarked, the men inside hadn't returned empty handed. The plastic shopping-bag could have contained just about anything, but the grenade launcher and gas-masks were definitely bad news. Doriot was not only determined to get inside the cave, he intended to make sure he didn't lose any more men doing so.

MARSEILLES, FRANCE

'You're sure you don't want me inside, covering your back?' Dixon asked.

'There's no need.'

Carrodus had finished checking the action of his revolver and was reloading the chambers.

'Don't underestimate Martel, whatever you do. He may be old but he hasn't softened with age.'

'He's a businessman. He'll see the light once I've shown him it's in his own best interests to co-operate.'

'OK, but be careful. I'll allow you an hour.'

Carrodus nodded and clambered out of the car. Le Chat Noir had been Martel's original headquarters, back in the days when he'd been establishing himself as the man to reckon with in Marseilles, and he'd never felt the need to move. As Carrodus knew, the club's tatty exterior was deceptive. It might resemble a score of other such establishments in the dock area but the interior had been converted into a fortress. Without an invitation there was very little chance of reaching Martel's office at the rear of the building.

Nevertheless, he had no doubts about Martel refusing to see him. He took the first step in the bar. After he'd paid for his drink, Carrodus told the barman what he wanted.

'Is Monsieur Martel expecting you?'

'No,' Carrodus admitted, 'but he'll still see me.'

Although he could speak perfect French, Carrodus was deliberately allowing his English accent to show. He couldn't afford any misunderstanding.

'I'll pass on your message but I wouldn't build up any hopes if I was you. He's a busy man.'

'Just tell him I visited the Flamingo and Pigalle last night. He'll find time.'

Five minutes later Carrodus was standing in front of Martel's desk. The two heavies behind him were a reminder that he wasn't a welcome guest.

'I don't like threats,' Martel said.

'Who's threatening?' Carrodus responded.

Threats were definitely a last resort.

'How else am I supposed to interpret the smoke bombs? The Pigalle had to close down for the night.'

Carrodus shrugged.

'They could easily have been incendiaries. Then both clubs would have been closed permanently. I was simply making sure you took me seriously.'

'I'm doing that all right.'

Martel's voice was grim.

'I hoped you might be.' Carrodus smiled pleasantly. 'Why not get rid of the hired help so we can talk? They took my gun before I came in here so you don't have anything to worry about.'

Martel was worried, and it irritated him not to know why.

'They stay,' he decided.

'In that case, I don't.' Carrodus made it sound as though walking out of the club would be the easiest thing in the world. 'What I have to say is for you alone. I'll give you one clue, though. There aren't any rubies. They never left Africa.'

This might have been a white lie but it persuaded Martel to change his mind. Only when the bodyguards were gone and he was seated did Carrodus allow himself to wipe the sweat from his palms. As he'd said to Dixon, the rest should be relatively straightforward. Martel was a businessman with his eyes on profits. It wouldn't be difficult to persuade him that it wasn't at all profitable to interfere in SR(2) affairs.

CHAPTER 14

I didn't like abandoning the shotgun but it was a necessary sacrifice. It was a weapon Doriot's men had every reason to respect and, as far as they knew, it was the only one we had. When they found the shotgun lying on the tunnel floor, this should help to convince them that we'd fled deeper into the hillside. I dragged the weapon along with me until it became a real encumbrance and then I dragged it a little further before I left it. I knew I was going to look awfully foolish if I'd miscalculated.

While I'd been busy with my disposal operation, Kuldip had taken over at the barricade.

'What's happening out there?' I asked once I'd rejoined her.

'There's been quite a lot of movement.' Although she was frightened, Kuldip had herself well under control. 'I make four men coming up the slope.'

After she'd pointed them out to me, I sent Kuldip back inside the cave. Doriot would be eager to get it over with and there was no point in both of us receiving the full benefits of the tear-gas or mace or CS gas or whatever. I wasn't particularly enthusiastic about hanging on till the last moment myself. Unfortunately, I had to make sure Doriot really was as predictable as I thought.

It was another quarter of an hour before the advancing group was close enough. When they were, the barrage started without any warning. I didn't spot a signal but suddenly there were half a dozen weapons blazing away at the cave entrance. Although they were deliberately shooting high, I hugged the floor until I was round the bend in the tunnel, then I was up and running.

The shooting was simply covering fire, and halfway to the crevice I heard the clatter as the first grenade arrived, followed almost immediately by a hissing sound as the gas was released. Fortunately, I could run faster than the gas could spread, even under pressure, and I spared time at the crevice opening to check that Kuldip was completely hidden. She was, but there wasn't anybody left to check on me. Once I'd squeezed in beside her, I had to pray I hadn't left any stray limbs sticking out.

Although I offered to put her to sleep for the duration, Kuldip wasn't interested. I'd told her what to expect but she preferred the discomfort to being unconscious while her fate was determined.

'OK,' I said, 'but don't make any mistake about it, it isn't going to be pleasant. The first sign of a cough or a splutter and I'm putting you out regardless.'

'How about you?' Fear didn't do a great deal for Kuldip's temper. 'What do I do if you cough and splutter?'

'I shan't,' I told her. 'I'm used to it.'

I ought to be. When you worked for SR(2), nobody tried to pretend you were in anything other than a high-risk occupation. Down at the training school, the instructors had made sure I'd had my four full sessions in the gas chamber, just like all the other graduates. This wasn't nearly enough exposure to develop any real immunity but it had shown me I could live with most of the common chemical agents.

I wasn't nearly so sure about Kuldip, but we proved to be lucky. Possibly we were too far from the cave entrance for the gas to be really effective. Or, more likely, perhaps the chimney acted like its more conventional namesake and sucked up most of the gas before it reached the crevice. Whatever the reason, our exposure was only minimal. Although I could tell Kuldip was suffering by the way she was squirming, she didn't make a sound. My own eyes were streaming and my nose was dripping like a leaky tap but this didn't inconvenience me sufficiently to stop me monitoring what was happening outside.

Three men had followed the tear-gas in, presumably the three with the gasmasks. They'd have been all psyched up, so the total lack of opposition must have been rather disconcerting, but they knew what they were doing. They maintained their momentum, driving on into the cave and hoping to overtake us before the effects of the gas had worn off. I heard them run past, then went back to listening to Kuldip's laboured breathing. Her face would be blotched and swollen, her eyes and nose would still be streaming but she'd weathered the worst. For once her pride and natural contrariness were working in my favour. After what I'd said, she'd rather die than admit I was a better man than she was.

The three men weren't in such a hurry on their way back. They hadn't gone all the way along the tunnel and they wouldn't have reached the point where I'd abandoned the shotgun. This wasn't their job. They were inside the cave and they'd dislodged us from our defensive position by the entrance. It wasn't down to them to chase us into the middle of the hillside. Once they were sure they hadn't overrun us, their part was finished.

It hadn't even occurred to me that they might overlook our crevice. It was far too obvious to miss and this was one of the things I'd been banking on. From the tunnel it seemed as though the whole of the small cavern was visible. It was only when you stepped right inside that the second opening became visible, the crevice within a crevice where Kuldip and I were huddling.

'Wait a minute,' a voice said outside.

They waited while a couple of torches played over the walls. I huddled a little closer to Kuldip and listened for the excited shouts which would signal discovery.

'It's a dead end and it's empty,' a second voice said. 'They must have gone straight down the tunnel.'

'Go inside and check,' the first voice told him. 'You know what Doriot's like so we'd better be sure.'

'Fuck Doriot.'

At least, this was what I thought the second man muttered, but I was too busy counting his footsteps as he moved into the outer cavern to be sure. Six paces were all I was prepared to allow him. Then I was going to shoot him, because on the seventh or eighth he'd see us and with two other men to handle I'd have to move fast. My count had reached five when the pool of light from his torch stopped growing any larger.

'We're wasting our time,' he said. 'Like I told you, it's empty.'

'OK. Let's go check the hole in the roof. Then Doriot can take over.'

For a minute or two after they'd gone, neither of us spoke. It was only when the sound of their voices had completely died away that Kuldip dared to break the silence.

'What do we do now?' she whispered.

'We stay where we are,' I said. 'Quietly.'

We might have bought ourselves a little more time but the basic situation remained the same. We were trapped and all the best cards were still in Doriot's hand.

During the next half-hour or so we heard plenty of movement backwards and forwards in the tunnel, together with some snatches of animated discussion, but we could only guess at what was happening. There was one particularly nasty moment when somebody stepped into the cavern with a torch. Whoever he was, he didn't bother us for long, contenting himself with a cursory flash round before he backed out again. After this we were in the dark again, both literally and figuratively, huddled together and feeling frightened. At least, this was how I felt, and I'd no reason to suppose Kuldip was any different.

We were also uncomfortable. Although the gas had cleared quickly, there were plenty of other annoyances. Sharp projections of rock dug into tender flesh, there wasn't quite enough floor for all our four feet to rest on at the same time, and so on. Worst of all, the lack of light was doing wonders for my claustrophobia and I could tell Kuldip wasn't any more at ease than I was. The little shifts of position and redistributions of weight were symptomatic.

According to my watch, we'd been in hiding for three quarters of an hour before the sounds of activity outside died away. I allowed another interminable quarter of an hour to tick away before I decided it was safe to speak.

'It's time we were thinking of a move,' I told Kuldip. 'Sooner or later, when we don't show up above ground, Doriot is going to check the cave again. He's likely to be more thorough the second time around.'

'So we make a break for it.'

Kuldip made it sound so simple that I took the time to explain exactly what we were up against. With the man-power at his disposal, Doriot could throw a cordon around the whole area and while we were inside it we were in trouble. If we'd had a definite timetable to work to, if we'd known the exact time when Martel would be calling his men off, it would have been worth the risk to try and stay under cover. As it was, I preferred to attempt to break through the cordon and any such break would have to be swift and decisive. The keys to the situation were the cars, and the chances were that they'd be guarded.

There were plenty of other potential hazards as well but none of them appeared to bother Kuldip. She'd undergone another of her mood swings. Fear had been replaced by excitement, and perhaps her enthusiasm was a good thing. If we did fail, she'd be facing reality soon enough.

Although we had to get out of the cave, there was no question of heading directly for the entrance. To begin with I didn't even allow Kuldip out of the crevice. During the hour or so we'd spent in the cleft, I'd had plenty of time to put myself in Doriot's place but assumptions had to be tested. About all I could be certain of was that he must have swallowed the bait. He should be convinced that the gas had driven us deeper into the hillside and, unless he was crazy, he wouldn't have sent his men in after us. There was no need when he knew we'd have to emerge somewhere.

However, one of the obvious places for us to emerge was back where we'd started and he might have left somebody behind in the cave. This was why I didn't rush myself as I went along the tunnel. I kept close to the left-hand wall, I watched out for loose rocks underfoot and I stopped to listen every few yards. It was all according to the textbook and the precautions were completely wasted. There was nothing, not even a shotgun lying on the ground.

When I retraced my footsteps, I didn't find anybody by the entrance either and I spent almost ten minutes standing in the shadows, scanning the hillside opposite. There was no sign of my friend with the rifle and this should have made me very happy but it didn't. Knowing where people weren't was useful, but I'd have far preferred to know exactly what arrangements Doriot had made. He was making things a little too easy for us. It was almost as though he was inviting me to try for the cars. If there'd been a telephone handy, I'd have been checking with Pawson to find out just how much longer I'd have to continue playing around in the Causses. As there wasn't one, I'd have to accept the invitation and I had an unpleasant suspicion that I'd be playing right into Doriot's hands.

By the time we were halfway to the cars I was positive that something was wrong. Kuldip had been running ahead of me, where I could keep an eye on her. Now I pulled level and signalled to her to stop.

'What's the matter?'

We'd both moved into the shelter of one of the larger rocks.

'Nobody has tried to stop us.'

We hadn't even heard any sounds of activity up on the plateau above the caves. Either Doriot had taken leave of his senses, his men had staged a lightning strike, or he knew as well as I did what his trump cards were. If his cordon was in place and the vehicles were covered, he didn't need anybody in the valley itself.

'From now on,' I said, 'I take the lead.'

Kuldip's shrug of acknowledgement didn't express any particular concern. Her mood was still on an upswing and now we were out of the cave she was behaving as though we were already home and dry. Luckily, I was more than capable of doing enough worrying for both of us.

When we set off again I changed course slightly, no longer heading directly for the area where the cars were parked. I was more concerned with keeping under cover and gaining a bit of height. Once I'd found a nice view-point, I settled down to a careful examination of the ground ahead. It all looked innocuous enough, without a soul in sight. At least, not anywhere near the cars. Now we were higher up I could see three figures moving up on the plateau above the caves but they were no immediate threat. They were too far away to take an active part in anything which happened.

There were, however, a couple of rock clusters which merited closer scrutiny. They were near enough to the vehicles to pose a potential threat and I'd have to check them out. Even so, it was largely a matter of going through the motions. Despite our progress to date, I refused to believe Doriot was as inefficient as he appeared to be. I still suspected we had as much hope of catching him on the hop as I had of running a three-minute mile.

Twenty minutes later I was seriously considering a re-vision of this opinion. I'd checked the two likely danger spots, along with half a dozen which weren't nearly so likely, and I hadn't found a thing. If I'd had a Bible handy, I'd have been prepared to swear on it that there wasn't a soul within a hundred yards of the cars apart from Kuldip and myself. It just didn't make sense.

I sat with my back against a rock, looking across the last few yards which separated us from the vehicles and going over my reasoning for the umpteenth time. Doriot hadn't been ordered off our backs because he still had men up on the plateau searching for us. In this case, there should have been men covering the valley and others watching the transport. There weren't and no matter how hard I tried I couldn't convince myself that this was the result of an oversight. It made me wonder exactly where the man with the rifle and telescopic sight had been moved to. The open area by the cars would make a perfect killing ground.

'What are we waiting for?' Kuldip asked.

She was hunkered down beside me. As far as she was concerned we were already free.

'I'm not sure,' I admitted. 'What's happening up on the plateau?'

'Nothing much.' It only took her a second to check over the top of the rock. 'They're still poking around in holes in the ground. Do we go now?'

'Why not?' Bad vibrations weren't sufficient to justify squatting behind the rock indefinitely and the cars remained our only realistic hope. If I'd been on my own, I'd have tried on foot. With Kuldip to worry about, this just wasn't on. 'We're taking the second Citroën, the one nearest the track. You go directly for the back door and once you're inside you stay down. I'm going to fix the other cars before I join you. OK?'

'Yes, master.'

Despite her flippancy, Kuldip's running was improving with practice and she was already tumbling into the Citroën as I reached the Peugeot at the head of the line. There was no time for anything elaborate and I restricted myself to one tyre per vehicle, stabbing with my knife until I'd punctured the inner tyre. This would only slow the pursuit a little, and it wouldn't do a thing about the damn helicopter, but it was the best I could manage.

While I was working my back muscles were tensed in anticipation of the rifle shot I'd never hear. Miraculously, it didn't come, not even when I dived into the driving seat of the Citroën. There were no signs of excitement up on the plateau, the keys were in the ignition and I couldn't believe it really was going to be this easy. When I tried the ignition, I knew it wasn't. The starter motor whirred away happily enough but this was all.

'Shi-i-it.'

I put all my pent-up frustration into the single obscenity.

'What's the matter?'

Kuldip's head had popped up over the back seat.

'Some bastard has been having a little joke at our expense. There's no rotor arm, so we won't be going anywhere. Stay where you are for a second.'

As high velocity bullets punched through metal almost as easily as they did through flesh and bone, it made very little difference whether I was inside the car or not. There was no immediate reaction to my reappearance and after a second I told Kuldip to join me. Her high spirits of a few minutes previously had completely evaporated.

'Philis . . .' she began.

She didn't finish, because Doriot had had his entertainment for the day. Now it was back to business.

The bullet hit the ground no more than nine inches from my left foot and I froze immediately, ignoring Kuldip's gasp of surprise. The warning couldn't possibly have been clearer and I didn't for a moment believe that the bullet had struck anywhere other than where it had been aimed.

'That's very good, Philis.' The loud-hailer distorted Doriot's voice too much for me to pinpoint exactly where he'd been hiding. 'Let's see just how far you can throw the gun and knife.'

I managed a pretty fair distance. Under the circumstances, they were no use to me and it was in my own best interests not to cause any waves. Talking to Doriot was about the only hope I had of staying alive.

'Both of you stay where you are. We're coming down to join you.'

While the two of them were working their way down the slope I thought of the little automatic Kuldip still had in her possession but I wasn't thinking very seriously. We were outgunned and we'd been outthought and the only thing I couldn't understand was why I hadn't been shot the moment I'd offered a clear target. This was something Doriot explained once he was with us. His sense of humour must have developed along the same lines as Caligula's.

'You have some work to do, Philis,' he told me. 'Don't bother about your car, but the other two need their wheels changing.'

'Ha, ha,' I said. 'Wouldn't it have been easier to stop me before I slashed the tyres?'

I probably sounded as sour as I felt. By contrast, Doriot's laugh was happy and carefree. It was the laugh of a winner.

'Possibly, but you've no idea how much I've been enjoying myself. I wanted to make sure you came back to earth with a real bang.'

I grunted my appreciation and started on the cars. I didn't bother to work very fast, despite Doriot's attempt to goad me into greater efforts, because I knew what would happen when I'd finished. However happy and carefree Doriot's laughter might have been, there'd been no mistaking the malice behind it. As soon as the cars were roadworthy again he was going to take great pleasure in killing me. I'd damaged his self-esteem back in Millau, and making a fool of me was only a small part of his revenge.

The only bright spot in a gloomy, and brief, future was that Pawson should have reached Martel by now, even if there had been no opportunity to pass the message on to Doriot. Unless the helicopter came flying in with a last-minute reprieve, which wasn't very likely, I'd have to rely on my silver tongue. I'd have to persuade Doriot to contact Martel before he carried out the standing orders, and this wasn't going to be easy. Doriot liked the standing orders. After all the aggravation I'd caused him, he wanted to kill me.

Although I spun out the wheel-changing for as long as possible I had to finish eventually and when I did Doriot was ready for me. He had a larger audience by now as the rest of his men had started to drift in and I realized what he intended to do when he called me over. Fists were much more personal than guns and I didn't mind him hitting me too much provided it helped him to work off some of his hostility. I needn't have gone down when I did, after Doriot had bounced his fists off my chin a couple of times, but it seemed like a good idea at the time. Doriot evidently disagreed. Two of his men hauled me back to my feet and propped me up while Doriot took a few more swings. He didn't punch his weight, but I didn't complain when he decided he'd had enough.

'That was for what happened in Millau,' he said, complacently rubbing his knuckles. 'The rest is simply business. I'm afraid we don't have room for you in either of the cars.'

While he was talking, Doriot pulled the automatic from its holster, a HK P9S with one of the polygon barrels. He was fiddling with the safety catch on the left side of the slide when I spoke.

'I wouldn't,' I said. 'You'd be making a bad mistake.'

To paraphrase one of the Irish comedians, it wasn't what you said, it was the way you said it. I made the trite words into a definitive statement, speaking with a quiet conviction I didn't feel.

'And why is that?'

'Because your Mr Martel wants me alive. I think you

ought to check with him before you try anything drastic.'

My confidence had unsettled Doriot but it was no more than a temporary success. I could tell when he started to shake his head.

'My orders were to dispose of you. Mr Martel told me not to bother to bring you back.'

'That was yesterday. The situation has changed since then.'

I kept on trying but I knew I'd lost the advantage and there was no hope of retrieving lost ground. The joke of it was, Doriot more than half-believed me. Unfortunately, he'd committed himself in advance. He wanted to kill me and Martel's standing orders gave him all the authority he needed.

'It was a nice try, Philis,' he said, 'but not quite good enough.'

This was the kind of aphorism which would look great on a tombstone. Although I desperately wanted to say something more, some magical new formula which would keep me intact into a ripe old age, my brain seemed to have stopped functioning. It was left to Kuldip to find the right words for me.

'Wait a minute,' she said.

And Doriot did. The interruption was so unexpected he even moved the automatic out of line with my head.

'I think I have a say in what happens to Philis,' Kuldip forged on.

'Why is that?'

Doriot couldn't keep the amazement out of his voice. In his milieu women knew their place.

'Because I'm the person this is all about. Philis has only been doing his job, trying to keep me safe.'

'How very commendable of him.' Doriot was openly laughing at her now. So were several of the other men who had arrived to swell our little group. 'I'd turn your head now, lady. I'm just about to do my job.'

'I wouldn't.' Kuldip handled the line even more convincingly than I had. She had the bit between her teeth by now and wasn't about to back down. 'I'm important to your Mr Martel. Very important, to judge by all the trouble he's gone to. Do you know why?'

'Not exactly.'

It was an admission Doriot hated to make.

'In that case, I'd better tell you.' The longer Doriot listened to her, the more Kuldip's confidence grew. I was having to stop myself from cheering her on. 'Your boss wants some information from me, information which will be worth a great deal of money to him. It's something I'm prepared to trade in return for a guarantee about our safety. Kill Philis, though, and there isn't going to be any trade. In fact, I shan't co-operate at all. I don't think that will make Mr Martel very happy.'

'I see.'

Doriot did, as well. There were far too many witnesses to what had been said for him to be able to ignore Kuldip. Nor was it any use his pointing out that the information could be squeezed out of her whether she co-operated or not. This wasn't a decision Doriot had any authority to make. I knew I was safe when he turned back to face me.

'It seems I'll have to find room for you after all,' he said savagely. 'Perhaps we can cram you into the boot.'

Then Doriot took two steps forward and hit me with his gun. I was unconscious before I could even start thinking that being hit was a hell of a sight better than being dead.

LONDON, ENGLAND

'You're slipping,' Kibunka said. 'You didn't frighten Philis enough.'

'I don't think I frightened him at all,' Kironde

answered. 'As I said at the time, Mr Philis wasn't at all what I'd expected.'

'That doesn't alter our problem. We haven't heard a thing from him since he left London.'

'I never thought we would.'

Kironde rose from his seat and walked across to the window. It was drizzling outside and the pavements were deserted apart from the two bodyguards who were huddled under the protection of one of the trees. Their presence was a constant irritant to him. He'd no intention of being as careless as Mukwaya.

'So what do we do now?' Kibunka asked. 'We're no closer to the woman than we were when we first arrived.'

'I wouldn't say that. Friend Philis told me more than he thought. He confirmed that she'd turned to Tenby for help and he told us that she's in France.'

'She may be in France,' Kibunka corrected him. 'If you remember, Philis wasn't sure who it was he was going to collect.'

'It's her.' Kironde's tone didn't leave any room for doubt. 'Best of all, we know Philis and Thackeray are bringing her to England.'

'On the other hand, Tenby must suspect he's being watched. When it matters, he's going to give us the slip.'

'With any luck, that may not be important any longer. That's why I wanted to see you.'

Now Kironde had turned from the window, Kibunka could see the faint smile on his lips.

'Come on,' he said. 'Don't drag it out any longer. Just tell me what you've heard.'

'It's something I've known for years but it wasn't important until a few days ago. That bitch we're looking for doesn't like flying. She has a positive phobia about it. She's physically incapable of going aboard an aeroplane, even if it means saving her life. And, in case you're still wondering, there's something called the Channel between

England and France.'

'You mean she'll be crossing by boat.'

Kibunka still couldn't understand the reason for all the excitement.

'Precisely. It took a lot of digging but Tenby wasn't quite as clever at hiding his tracks as he thought. She'll be travelling aboard a boat called *The Mallard*.'

'Do you know where it is?'

Now the excitement had communicated itself to Kibunka as well.

'At the moment it's moored at a little port called Cavalière-sur-Mer. I thought we might take a trip across to France. How do you fancy becoming the first Ugandan pirate?'

After Kironde had finished explaining, Kibunka liked the idea very much indeed.

CHAPTER 16

'Philis.'

The voice seemed to be coming from a long way away and I didn't pay it a great deal of attention. However, when the owner of the voice began slapping my face, I did react. My head hurt enough already without it being swatted around any more.

'Stop it,' I mumbled.

'Come on, Philis. Snap out of it.'

There was a note of impatience in the voice now. This, together with a couple more slaps, persuaded me to force my eyelids apart. For a few seconds I was looking out at a vaguely surrealist world, with everything fuzzy around the edges. Then the dizziness passed and I could recognize Kuldip leaning over me. There wasn't much in the way of tender concern on her face, and her right hand was going

back for another slap. I used one hand to block her little
display of affection and the other to explore the top of my
head. Although it was tender to the touch, there weren't
any readily identifiable dents.

'You'd make a great nurse,' I said. 'You have that
gentle bedside manner.'

'Very funny.' The impatience was still there. 'How do
you feel?'

'I'm just fine apart from the concussion, double vision and
fractured skull.' I demonstrated this by lifting myself higher
on the pillows, a manoeuvre which didn't quite send the top
of my skull into orbit. 'What's been happening?'

Nothing much, was the answer. Doriot and his merry
men had driven us down off the Causses to where we were
now, shut up in a bedroom. About all Kuldip could tell
me was that we were in some kind of farmhouse. This was
something I'd already deduced for myself. The cackling
of chickens and the subtle scent of decaying pig-shit
weren't features I'd ever associated with the Ritz.

Sitting up was considerably less painful than I'd anticipated and I managed to stand without any assistance
from Kuldip. I only had to hobble a couple of steps to the
dirt-grimed window and it wasn't a profitable journey.
There was a small, untidy yard below, complete with the
expected chickens and a pile of pig droppings. I could
even see a couple of the porkers who had helped to pro-
duce the manure but none of the landmarks beyond the
farmyard struck any chord in my memory.

After I'd lurched back to the bed, I tried Kuldip with a
few more questions. Doriot had driven off almost immediately after our arrival at the farmhouse, presumably
to establish contact with Martel. Although Kuldip was
unable to tell me exactly where the remaining men were
posted, this wasn't really important. There was no sense in
doing anything until Doriot had returned. Pawson should
have reached Martel by now but it wouldn't matter too

much even if he'd been dragging his feet. Thanks to Kuldip, there was no immediate threat to our health or welfare.

My chain of thought reminded me that I hadn't had an opportunity to express my appreciation of what Kuldip had done for me, an omission I attempted to remedy now. Although I probably phrased my gratitude clumsily, the sentiments got across.

'Forget it.' Kuldip was actually embarrassed. 'You've done the same for me more than once. Besides, my motives weren't entirely unselfish.'

'Never.'

I couldn't suppress my smile and Kuldip aimed a mock punch at me.

'I'm used to having you around to bail me out of trouble,' she said, 'and I need you more than ever now. Unless you manage to come up with something, we're both going to be killed.'

'Quite frankly, I don't give a tinker's damn what your motives were.' For once, I was being completely honest. 'You saved my life and that isn't something I'm likely to forget in a hurry.'

Kuldip was visibly pleased, which was the whole object of the exercise. There were occasions when I could be quite a nice guy.

As soon as I saw Doriot's face, I knew Pawson had been pulling his strings. The Frenchman looked like a dog who had lost his favourite bone and I celebrated his return by sitting up on the edge of the bed while Kuldip struck a dramatic pose over by the window. My head was feeling much better by now and I produced a fair approximation of a smile.

'Let me guess,' I said. 'You've been having words with Martel.'

'I have.'

No matter what his new instructions might be, Doriot's personal attitude towards me hadn't changed at all.

'In that case you ought to be thanking us. Just think of all the trouble you'd be in if you'd killed me.'

'It might have been worth it.' Doriot sounded totally sincere. 'Mr Martel apologizes for the misunderstanding and inconvenience and says you're free to go. You have his personal assurance that you'll be perfectly safe during the remainder of your stay in France.'

'You're saying we can go?' Kuldip demanded. 'Just like that?'

She'd never had a great deal of faith in Sir Keith's ability to pull our chestnuts out of the fire.

'That's correct.'

'We can simply walk out of here?'

'We're not walking anywhere.' I'd intervened to save Doriot any more pain. 'One of our hosts is going to fetch our car for us. He's even going to wash the dust off and change the wheel. While that's being done, Doriot here is going to supervise a meal for us. Isn't that right?'

Doriot seemed to be afraid that his head might fall off if he shook it too hard and his answering nod of the head was almost imperceptible. He didn't even trust himself to speak, preferring to turn on his heel and start off down the stairs. Unlike him, I was a gentleman and I ushered Kuldip out of the door ahead of me.

'How the hell did Sir Keith manage it?' she whispered fiercely. 'What did he say to Martel?'

'That's something you'll have to ask him. For the moment let's eat, drink and make merry.'

This seemed a lot easier than fabricating any more lies.

The drive through France was almost a holiday. Now the pressure was off we could afford to relax and I spread the journey over three days, choosing a route which gave us plenty of scenery and no hassle. The sex was good, we laughed a lot and we generally enjoyed ourselves. Kuldip put her petulance into cold storage, I was heavy-handed with the flattery and attentiveness and it was all very pleasant. If either of us had been able to really trust the other, it might have been more than pleasant.

On the third evening, I left Kuldip in the hotel in Le Havre and drove on ahead. My destination, Cavalière-sur-Mer, proved to be little more than a marina. There'd once been a fishing village on the site, based on toil not leisure, but the dozen or so grey stone cottages had become no more than a quaint reminder of the past. The village had been converted into a nautical garage cum parking lot. When I arrived there were about thirty boats moored in the harbour, a mixture of cruisers and yachts. On shore there were about twice as many people loitering around, showing off suntans, muscles or boobs depending on their sex and inclination.

Most of them were clustered around the marina's control centre, a complex containing shops, a restaurant and the harbour office. There was also a bar and this was where I headed. It was as good a place as any to ask some questions and I'd already spotted *The Mallard*, a roomy two-masted fifty-footer parked out at the end of one of the jetties.

Inside the bar I took care to find myself a bar stool which effectively isolated me from the rest of the customers. En masse, weekend sailors gave me an acute pain in the buttock region, as did similar groups of gravediggers, brain surgeons and Afghan astronauts. I didn't care about not belonging to their exclusive brotherhood, or not being able to understand more than one word in four of what they were saying, but I was a maverick. I didn't have any nice slot to fit into and I had a vague contempt for the group mentality. As Dr Lunt invariably pointed out in his six-monthly evaluation, this was much better for me than admitting that there might be any flaws or inadequacies in my own make-up.

However, there was a more practical motive for my isolation. The person I wanted to talk to was the slow-moving

Frenchman behind the bar. He wasn't noticeably more en-
tranced by the clientele than I was, a useful basis for what I
hoped to discuss. After I'd bought him a couple of drinks, his
Anglophobe tendencies evaporated and he became quite
amiable. To begin with I kept our conversation general but,
once I'd established he was a fisherman of sorts, it wasn't difficult to prod him in the direction I wanted. He proved to
have strong, and decidedly obscene, opinions about some of
the idiots who messed about on the sea in boats. He regaled
me with a couple of true stories to emphasize his point, then I
threw in my fictitious one.

'Just wait until the Ugandans get here,' I said.

'The Ugandans?'

Hardly surprisingly, Henri didn't have the foggiest idea
what I was talking about.

'There's a whole boatload of them pottering around the
Channel this summer,' I explained. 'They're supposed to be
affiliated to the Kampala Yacht Club or some such non-
sense. I'd guess that their only previous experience was pad-
dling canoes on Lake Victoria. Over in Margate, they had to
be rescued three times before they'd even left harbour.'

Although Henri seemed to be quite amused, there was
no positive reaction, which there should have been if he'd
been in contact with any Ugandans himself. Cavalière
was too small for a group of Africans to blend in with the
local scenery. There was a brief break in our conversation
when Henri moved down the bar to serve another gaggle
of would-be Sir Francis Chichesters. I celebrated his return
by buying him another drink and trying a different tack.

'I was hoping to find a friend of mine in here,' I said, 'A
man called Scargill.'

'You mean from *The Mallard*?'

I nodded.

'You'll probably find him on board,' Henri told me.
'He and his son are professional sailors. They don't mix
much with the crowd in here. I've hardly seen anything of

them the last few days. One or other of them pops ashore occasionally to pick up supplies but they prefer to keep themselves to themselves.'

This was an attitude Henri evidently approved of. Although I persevered with him for another five minutes, he didn't have anything more to say. The bar was becoming busier as well, as more of the yachtsmen came in for their evening tot, so I excused myself and took my drink to a table by the window where I could watch *The Mallard*. It was almost dark now and all I had to watch was the outline of the boat, together with the occasional glow when somebody puffed at a cigarette on deck.

To judge by what Henri had had to say, Scargill was behaving exactly the way Thackeray had said he would. He was waiting in the appointed place and he was sticking close to the boat, ready to cast off the moment he had some passengers to transport across the Channel. On the other hand, I'd telephoned London again immediately after Doriot had released us. In the light of one piece of information Pawson had given me, Scargill's behaviour was open to a different interpretation. Henri hadn't seen Scargill and his son together over the past few days. 'One or other of them' had come ashore to buy supplies. This could simply show how conscientious they were. Alternatively, it could signify something else, and this was why I'd come on ahead to Cavalière-sur-Mer.

It was pleasant to escape the smoke and hubbub of the bar and I took my time as I strolled along the jetty. Whoever it was who had been on deck was no longer smoking and I walked straight past *The Mallard*, going to the very end of the jetty. It was my turn for a cigarette and I smoked a Senior Service all the way down before I turned my back on the sea and started back. On the return trip, however, I wasn't allowed to walk past *The Mallard*.

'That's far enough, Philis,' the man said. 'Just stay where you are.'

It was a voice I knew. I recognized the shotgun, as well, when it emerged from the shadows.

'I thought you might be here,' I said. 'Pawson told me you'd left for France.'

For the moment at least, Kironde wasn't at all interested in who Pawson might be. All he wanted was to get me aboard the boat without any fuss.

LONDON, ENGLAND

After his secretary had gone, Sir Keith Tenby reread the brief message. It was a telegram he had been awaiting with increasing anxiety for the past few days. Now it had eventually arrived, he wasn't quite sure what to make of it. Although there were only four words, put into the simple code he'd arranged with Thackeray, the implication was that something must have gone drastically wrong. First there had been the delay, and then the telegram was signed 'PHILIS', not 'THACKERAY' as it should have been. Against this, the main text read 'ON OUR WAY'. This suggested that any difficulties had become a thing of the past.

As he refolded the slip of paper and put it into his pocket, Sir Keith hoped that his assumptions about Thackeray were incorrect. He knew it would be almost impossible to find an adequate replacement for him. On the other hand, it was a distinct relief to know that Philis still had the Ugandan woman with him. His various companies' investments in black Africa ran into scores of millions of pounds and they'd most certainly be at risk if the exact nature of his dealings with Amin ever became public knowledge. When it came to the bottom line, the shareholders were infinitely more important than any employee, no matter how efficient he might have been.

CHAPTER 17

'We're both more or less on the same side of the fence,' Pawson had said. 'There's no need for any confrontation. If Kironde does get in your way, work something out with him.'

This had sounded marvellous at the time and I'd been all in favour of the idea. Unfortunately, it had contained one basic flaw. Kironde thrived on confrontation. He didn't want to sort anything out. All he wanted was Kuldip and he wasn't fussy about the means he used to reach her.

As far as I could tell, there were four Ugandans on board. Two of them were keeping an eye on the captive Scargills and the other two were in the main cabin with me. Of the two, I'd have far preferred to be negotiating with Kibunka. On short acquaintance, he struck me as a reasonable man, not a bloodthirsty fanatic like Kironde, and we could soon have reached a satisfactory compromise. Sad to say, though, he was very much the junior partner. Although he did voice the odd objection, it was what Kironde said which carried weight.

This was why I was beginning to sweat. I'd explained that I worked for SR(2), not Sir Keith. I'd said that the department's interest in Kuldip was purely peripheral. Our target was Sir Keith and once we had him tied up, Kironde was welcome to any other pickings. And Kironde still didn't want to play. He seemed to operate on a plane beyond reason and he didn't give a damn who I worked for. If I stood in between him and Kuldip, I was likely to get crushed.

'Look,' I said, being as reasonable as I always was when I was talking to somebody with a shotgun. 'At this precise moment, I'm the only person who knows where Kuldip is. It isn't information I intend to share until we've reached an agreement.'

'Perhaps I can persuade you to change your mind.'

We both knew what Kironde was talking about and he was in deadly earnest.

'Long live Amin,' I said ironically. 'Your brave, new Uganda should be a vast improvement.'

'I only do what I have to.'

'Sure.' Respect for the shotgun was beginning to fade the more Kironde got up my nose. 'Wasn't that Idi's rationale as well?'

I could afford a limited amount of disrespect. As I explained to Kironde, I wasn't particularly brave and I certainly wasn't a fool. I knew from past experience that if somebody hurt me, I yelled and screamed just like everybody else. If I was hurt enough, I could be persuaded to tell people anything they wanted to hear. This was why I went to such lengths to avoid situations where I was likely to be hurt and why my instructions to Kuldip had been explicit. I had just twenty-five minutes left before I had to telephone her. Miss this deadline and she'd book out of her hotel without leaving a forwarding address. Even I wouldn't know where she was. Kironde might be able to squeeze me dry but this wouldn't leave him nearly enough time to reach Kuldip before she headed for the hills. It wasn't enough to make Kironde throw in the towel.

'There is one possible shortcut,' he told me, casually hefting his damn shotgun in one hand.

'You think so?'

'Certainly. I doubt whether you're prepared to die for the bitch, whoever you work for. Either you tell me what I need to know or I'll blow your head off.'

'You can't do that.'

The objection had come from Kibunka and carried my wholehearted endorsement.

'I can and I will. You have exactly two minutes, Philis. Then I'm going to shoot you.'

'Where will that leave you?'

'Looking at your dead body.' This wasn't a prospect which appeared to worry Kironde as much as it did me. 'Nobody asked you or your department to meddle in Ugandan affairs and you have to face the consequences. Your two minutes start now.'

Kironde might be a certifiable maniac but his time limit was very nicely judged. The traditional count of ten didn't allow a potential victim an opportunity to absorb the full impact of what was about to happen to him. It took a conscious effort for me to tear my eyes away from the business end of the shotgun and look across at Kibunka. By then I'd already visualized pieces of the noble Philis head being splattered to all four corners of the cabin. If Kironde did carry out his threat, anybody interested in my death mask would have to be bloody good at jigsaw puzzles.

The manner in which Kibunka avoided my eyes didn't do a thing to reassure me. He clearly wasn't enjoying what was happening and he seemed genuinely shocked by the turn of events but he wasn't about to intervene. As for Kironde, his expression was absolutely implacable. I'd already watched him gun down two men without turning a hair and I failed to see why he should feel any differently about me.

'You have ninety seconds, Philis,' he said.

I resisted the temptation to glance down at my wrist-watch and decided he wasn't bluffing. It didn't matter to him whether I worked for SR(2), Alcoholics Anonymous or the Gas Board. In his own warped mind, Kironde had right on his side and anybody who stood in his way deserved to be eliminated. As far as he was concerned, it was all or nothing. Either I cracked and gave him an outside chance of reaching Kuldip in time or I didn't. And if I didn't, he might just as well kill me because I'd have become nothing more than an unwanted nuisance.

'One minute,' Kironde said.

Perhaps I was being too pessimistic. However inflexible

Kironde might be, however alien compromise might be to his nature, he was intelligent enough to realize that half the cake was better than no cake at all. Kill me and he'd lost Kuldip. While I was alive, a deal was still possible. Then again, whatever his other defects, Kironde was no wanton killer. He saw himself as a man of principle and he killed for what he considered necessity, not for pleasure. If he failed to break me, killing me would be pointless. It would simply compound his failure.

'Forty-five seconds.'

Time to scrap at least one of my grounds for hope. Fear and stress were muddling my thinking and I was applying a yardstick to Kironde which wasn't relevant because our concepts of necessity probably didn't have much in common. Kironde was a fanatic in the true sense of the word. No matter how high-flown he might consider the moral basis of his crusade, he didn't really give a damn for what happened to his fellow countrymen. Otherwise he'd have been back in Uganda helping to sort out the mess Amin had left behind. Kironde's motive was revenge pure and simple. His self-appointed mission was to eliminate anybody tainted by contact with Amin and I was probably guilty by association. I was in his way and this placed me squarely among the ranks of the enemy.

'Half a minute.'

I could also scrap the belief that Kironde would be forced to deal with me if I held out. He believed in doing things his way and he'd managed to reach *The Mallard* without any help from me. Kuldip would still be heading for Sir Keith and Kironde might consider this was all he needed to know. He might decide to make another attempt to intercept her on the far side of the Channel. He'd already made it patently obvious that he wasn't looking for allies, especially not SR(2).

'You have just ten seconds left to start talking.'

Now we were down to the traditional count of ten and I

still wasn't any closer to reading Kironde's mind. It was
time to abandon surmise in favour of gut-think. Kironde
didn't look as though he was bluffing and I'd no intention
of dying, either for Kuldip or Pawson. All I had to do was
mention the name of a hotel in Le Havre and I'd be safe.

'Five,' Kironde said. 'Four, three . . .'

It was Kibunka who saved me the need to reach a decision. I'd been monitoring his struggle with his conscience
and, belatedly, he made up his mind. The automatic
came out of his waistband, he took two steps forward and
the muzzle of the gun was pressing against the back of
Kironde's head.

'Put the shotgun down,' he ordered, his voice strained.
'Now.'

I didn't start feeling grateful to Kibunka until after
Kironde had obeyed him. The shock of having a gun held
to his head could easily have made Kironde squeeze the
trigger and this wasn't something I'd have enjoyed at all.

'It's all right,' Kironde said, the mad look gone from his
eyes. 'I never had any intention of shooting Philis.'

'Of course you didn't.' The shake in my voice didn't do
a lot for my sarcasm. 'You're a humanitarian at heart.'

Kironde actually allowed himself the glimmer of a
smile as he shook his head. In his sane moments he was
probably quite likeable.

'It wasn't that, Philis. Kill you and I'd have had to kill
both of the Scargills to cover myself. I'm not in the market
for massacres.'

For the life of me, I couldn't tell whether he was joking
or not.

Now he'd finished playing silly buggers, Kironde was
co-operation itself. I left *The Mallard* briefly to telephone
Kuldip and tell her all was well. Then it was time for a
few cards to be laid on the table. As Pawson still hadn't
taken me into his confidence, most of the cards came

from Kironde's hand. Some of what he had to say I already knew and some of it I'd guessed, but Kironde put it all together for me in one neat package.

The key to everything was that Kuldip had been Amin's mistress for the last three years of his rule. Although this was by no means an exclusive position, Kuldip had possessed qualities which had set her apart from the opposition. She was intelligent, as well as ambitious, and, for some strange reason, Amin had trusted her. Gradually, over the months, the nature of their relationship had changed. From being a nice little piece on the side, Kuldip had progressed to becoming the President's personal assistant, handling those matters which were too confidential to be entrusted to anybody else. While she never had any official standing, Kuldip had probably known more about what was really going on in Uganda than anyone apart from Amin himself.

This was why she was so important to Kironde. At the end, when Amin's downfall had become inevitable, the more important of his select band of cronies had begun to think to their futures. They knew what they'd have to answer for. They knew how many enemies they'd made. What they had wanted were completely new identities which would leave them secure from retribution while they enjoyed the plunder from the good years.

It was one of the jobs which had been handed to Kuldip. She'd dealt with the documentation and travel arrangements for those deemed worthy of such treatment and these were the very men Kironde most wanted. Amin himself might be safe for the moment, living in a luxury hotel at Jidda in Saudi Arabia, but his henchmen were more vulnerable provided Kironde knew their new identities. Kuldip was the one person who knew where they all were.

Her value to Sir Keith was totally different. Although Kironde didn't know enough of the details to give me the whole picture, it was clear enough for all that. Sir Keith's

dealings with Amin weren't something he'd want to boast
about. In view of his massive holdings in other parts of the
continent, it could be most damaging for them to become
public knowledge. It was reasonable to assume that these
transactions were something else Kuldip must have handled
for Amin, either that or she'd had access to the records of
them. As Kironde pointed out, this was the only logical
explanation for the lengths Sir Keith had gone to in order
to protect her. Kuldip had turned to him when she'd
found herself in trouble and she must have had a pretty
potent lever to persuade him to respond so promptly.

'That's the part I don't understand,' I said. 'How did
Kuldip get herself in such a mess? There she was at
Amin's right hand, the one person he really trusted, yet
she didn't go with him to Libya. What happened? Did
Amin decide to ditch her?'

'What you don't understand, Philis, is the woman
herself.' Throughout his explanation Kironde had never
once referred to Kuldip by name. 'She's ruthless, she's
ambitious and she's exclusively self-centred. She was the
one who did the ditching. It was all very nice while she
was the unofficial first lady in Kampala, but being an ex-
President's mistress wouldn't have been nearly so much
fun. She decided to strike out on her own and that's where
the rubies come in.'

I'd been wondering when they'd eventually receive a
mention, and nothing Kironde had to say on the subject
cast Kuldip in a better light. As Kironde admitted, he
wasn't sure whether she'd been acting as Amin's courier
or off her own initiative. All that he could be certain of
was that she'd come to an arrangement with one of the
most unsavoury officers in the SRB, a James Onyoro. Like
all the best agreements, it had been firmly rooted in
mutual self-interest. Onyoro had been one of the very first
to flee from Uganda and Kuldip had needed him to find a
market for the rubies abroad. In turn, Onyoro had needed

Kuldip because she was the one person with the authority to walk into the mine and liberate the rubies. All proceeds were to be split straight down the middle.

To begin with it had all gone very well. Kuldip had obtained the rubies, she'd smuggled them out of Uganda and she'd met Onyoro. After this, things had only gone well for Onyoro. Either Kuldip had been very naive, which seemed most unlikely, or the safeguards she'd incorporated into the deal hadn't been safe at all. It didn't really matter which, because the outcome was a matter of history. Onyoro had walked off with several million dollars' worth of rubies and Kuldip had been left with nothing.

The little I knew of Kuldip made the next step entirely predictable. Although the rubies had been lost, she'd still been determined to have her revenge, and the new government in Kampala had received a communication revealing the new identities of Onyoro and the three other men who had assisted him in the rip-off. This had been a grave error of judgment on Kuldip's behalf. She would have been far better advised to have forgotten her losses and concentrated on her future.

Although Kironde's men had quickly located Onyoro's three associates, Onyoro himself had anticipated Kuldip's reaction to the double-cross. While he'd been arranging a market for the stones he'd also been arranging yet another new identity for himself, and Kironde had no idea of his present whereabouts. However, before Onyoro had dropped out of sight, he'd had one last parting gift for Kuldip, hinting to several of his ex-colleagues that their futures might be more secure if Kuldip was out of the way. Hence the determined efforts to eliminate her and Kuldip's subsequent appeal to Sir Keith.

'I'm confused,' I said. 'One of the Ugandans who was looking for Kuldip was grabbed by Martel in Marseilles. He said that she still had the rubies.'

Kironde shrugged.

'Onyoro was protecting himself and making sure they went after Kuldip at the same time. Ex-colleagues or not, he wasn't about to admit that he'd just become a millionaire.'

This left only one minor point to be explained.

'You seem to be remarkably well-informed,' I said. 'How do you know so much about what went on?'

'Onyoro's three associates haven't been my only successes.' Kironde's smile wasn't a pretty one. 'We've managed to track down most of the small fry. One or two of them have even been captured alive.'

'And they co-operated?'

'With a little bit of persuasion.'

I could imagine. Now Kironde had pulled most of the pieces together for me, it only remained to sort out the terms of our arrangement. From where I was sitting it all seemed pretty straightforward. Kironde and company could head back to London, I'd lean on the Scargills a little to ensure they kept their mouths closed aboard *The Mallard* and then I'd escort Kuldip across the Channel. I'd no idea of Pawson's plans but I did know Kuldip would have to be taken into custody at some stage of the operation and Kironde would receive his reward after she'd been debriefed. As I told him, we'd lost Mortenson in Kampala in '76, so there'd be no question of Pawson being reluctant to pass on any relevant information.

Unfortunately, this wasn't good enough for Kironde. Relevant information wasn't the only thing he was after.

'I want the woman.' He made this a demand rather than a request. 'I don't mind Pawson having first crack at her but when he's finished she's to be handed over to me.'

'Is that really necessary?' I made the mistake of thinking Kironde was simply being awkward. 'Access to the tapes of her interrogation is the best I can manage. I just don't have the authority to offer any more.'

'In that case we're wasting our time. Unless I get the woman there's no deal.'

Belatedly I realized that there had to be something more. The malevolence in Kironde's voice was almost frightening in its intensity.

'OK, I'll get back to Pawson. I'm going to need some form of justification, though.'

'Believe me, I can give you all the justification you need.'

I didn't get it straight away because Kironde was unable to continue immediately. Instead he rose to his feet and walked across to the far side of the cabin, stopping with his back to me. I'd have had to be blind not to have realized that Kironde was somebody who lived on emotion, but his present state was something else again. He was so distraught I wished Kibunka hadn't left us alone. If Kironde had to be restrained, I'd probably need help.

'That bitch,' Kironde said, almost spitting the words out, 'was no virgin when Amin met her. She had to work her way up the ladder rung by rung, or perhaps I should say bed by bed. Mine was one of the first beds on the way. She was my mistress for almost a year and I was the fool who took her from Jinja to Kampala.'

Kironde was becoming so overcharged he had to stop for a moment. Although he still had his back to me, he positively radiated tension.

'Go on,' I prompted quietly. 'I'm listening.'

'My only excuse was that I was young and she made me feel more of a man than any other woman I'd ever met.' The intensity remained but now it was almost as though Kironde was talking to himself. 'My marriage was arranged for me. We became fond of one another, of course, but at the time it was duty, nothing more. I was eighteen then and I didn't know another woman until I was posted to Jinja. Apart from the occasional whore, that is, and they didn't count. I didn't have the experience to realize that that bitch was nothing more than a different kind of whore. I was totally infatuated with her. She was my first great passion and I was naive enough to believe she felt the same about me. It didn't even occur to me that I was being used.'

He was forced to pause again. The words might come straight from the pages of a cheap romance but the emotions behind them were frighteningly real.

'I trusted her,' Kironde went on. 'Can you believe it, I actually trusted her. I shared secrets with her that I didn't even tell my wife or father. I was so blinded with desire, so immersed in the pleasures of her body, that I couldn't see what kind of a weapon I was giving her.'

'And she betrayed you.'

'Betrayed me?' Kironde's short bark of laughter was entirely devoid of humour. 'She did more than that. She helped to destroy everything in life that was dear to me. You see, she'd already set her sights on the next rung of the ladder. He was a colonel in the SRB, one of Amin's right-hand men, and she didn't go to him empty-handed. I'd warned her that my father and I were plotting against the government and that if things did go wrong she might be in trouble. Her in trouble, can't you see the joke of it? She gave her new lover every last detail of the plot to overthrow Amin and that's why I intend to have her now. She has the blood of my entire family on her hands. Is that justification enough for your Mr Pawson?'

I guessed it was more than enough but, despite what I'd just heard, I couldn't help feeling a certain sympathy for Kuldip. Kironde had turned around when he'd phrased his question and, no matter what Kuldip had been responsible for in the past, nobody deserved the fate I could read in his face.

Kuldip was waiting up for me when I eventually arrived back at the hotel, modelling the ridiculous white negligee she'd picked up on the trip north. She welcomed me with a kiss which had more to do with relief than affection.

'I was getting worried,' she said.

'I don't see why. I'm a big boy now. I've been going out

on my own for months.'

'But you were so long. What went wrong?'

'I succumbed to the demon drink. I've been sampling our captain's range of duty-free beverages.'

'I thought I could smell it on your breath.' Kuldip had remained within grappling range. 'Is it all fixed? Did you arrange when we leave?'

'We go tomorrow morning. I told Scargill to expect us aboard some time after breakfast. With any luck we should be in England by the afternoon.'

'That's nice.' Kuldip gave a little grind of her pelvis against me. 'It gives us one last night together.'

'Don't build up too many hopes,' I told her. 'I was planning to sleep.'

'There'll be plenty of time for that on the boat.' Kuldip moved against me again, more provocatively on this occasion. 'Surely you're not getting tired of me already.'

'Now you mention it, it has been getting a bit routine.' I accompanied this with a grin, just to make sure Kuldip realized I was joking. 'The problem is, I've never been able to mix booze and sex. After my little session with Scargill, I'm going to be suffering from a terminal case of distiller's droop.'

'Pig,' Kuldip said.

Although she'd made the ritual protest, Kuldip wasn't noticeably upset by the rejection. Like so many before me, I was a rung she'd already used on the ladder. This time it was different, though. What Kuldip didn't realize was that now she was travelling downwards, into the depths.

Ritchie Perry was born in King's Lynn, England, and educated at St. John's College, Oxford. He has traveled widely in Europe and Latin America, and currently resides in Bedfordshire, where he is a primary school teacher.

Other books in the Philis series by Ritchie Perry include: *The Fall Guy, A Hard Man to Kill, Ticket to Ride, Holiday with a Vengeance, Your Money and Your Wife, One Good Death Deserves Another, Bishop's Pawn,* and *Grand Slam.*